Gabrielle Kent

KNIGHTS AND BIKES

WHEELS OF LEGEND

Illustrated by Rex Crowle

and Luke Newell

"Based on the Knights And Bikes
video game by Foam Sword. OUT NOW!"

KO
KNIGHTS OF

Map of Penfurzy

THE SCRAPYARD

AVALON'S PEAK
CARAVAN PARK

THE GOLF COURSE

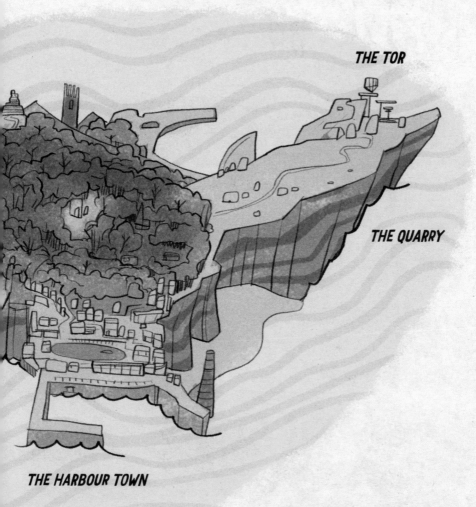

THE TOR

THE QUARRY

THE HARBOUR TOWN

Gabrielle: For Ashoka, Caitriona, Caiden, Ramy, Jodhi, Zain, Nate and Alba

Luke: For Claire, Vera and Iris

CONTENTS PAGE

Chapter One
INVASION OF THE SNOT GOBLINS

"Monsters!" screamed Demelza, as she peered between the flowery curtains of her little caravan with one eye.

Honk! her pet goose, Captain Honkers, squawked from under her armpit, as he poked his head through the curtains next to hers.

"Look at them, Honkers. Drooling, screaming, stinky invaders! They're **EVERYWHERE!** We're surrounded and Nessa's on her way up the hill... she'll never make it through the horde!"

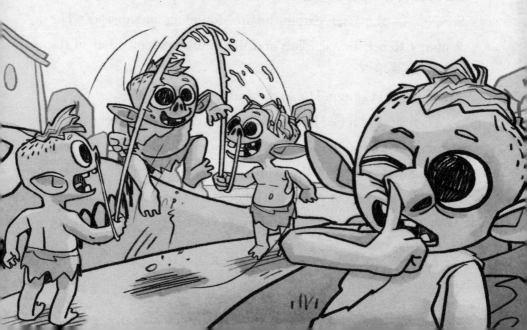

HONK! Captain Honkers couldn't contain his fury any longer. He wriggled out from under her arm and ran around the caravan flapping his wings, knocking books, toys and crayons off the shelves. **Honk-HONK!**

"You're right," shouted Demelza. "They shall not defeat us! We're going out there! We'll fight our way through to Nessa." She stood tall and placed her hand on her chest. "For she is our bestest friend. She'd do the same for us." She grabbed two foam swords from under the bed and slotted them through the straps on the back of her dungarees. Pulling her Game Gauntlet out from under her pillow she slid it onto her hand and made a fist.

"Ready, Captain?" she asked her goose. "Will you brave the rabid horde with me and risk your life, NAY… your very SOUL, to save Sir Nessa, trespasser extraordinaire, founding member of The Penfurzy Rebel Bicycle Club and the awesomest spit sister in the history of spit?"

Honk? said Captain Honkers, head tilted to one side.

"Then let's go!" cried Demelza. She kicked the door of her caravan open and braced herself against the overwhelming shrieking, cackling, shouting and singing of the army of monsters. She pulled out her swords, took a deep breath and leapt down the steps with a roar:

"Penfurzy Rebel Bicycle Club to the rescue! For one, for all, for Nessaaaaaa!"

She brandished a sword in each hand as she edged her way through the caravan park, waving her weapons warningly at any invaders that came too near. Some of the larger ones were lounging around jabbering to each other, or scratching their big sweaty stomachs and hairy backs, as the smaller ones ran wildly around, shrieking and drooling, snot dripping from their noses. Far in the distance Demelza could see Mr Calenick – the pickled knight, caravan park caretaker and former beheaded Penfurzy Knight - riding his new lawnmower around the crazy golf course. The horde hadn't breached that field yet, but he was too far away to hear her call for help. She had to make it through alone.

"Raaaargh!" shouted a snot goblin, charging at Demelza with a handful of worms.

Hissssssss! Captain Honkers spat so loudly that the little monster fell over in fright, scattering worms everywhere.

"Hah! Nice try!" Demelza shouted, as the monster scooted away from them on its bum. "Maybe little girls are scared of worms where you come from, but here…" she gave him a very wide, very toothy grin, "we eats worms for breakfast. Isn't that right, Honkers?"

HONK! Captain Honkers pounced on the worms and gobbled up as many as he could fit in his beak.

3

"Nessa! shouted Demelza, "Look Honkers, here she comes!" Nessa did a little hop on her back wheel as she wheelied through the gates of the caravan park on her shining steed, Neon Justice II.

"Nessa, stop!" Demelza shouted, swerving to avoid a hairy lumbering beast as it thundered past her to stop a fight between two shrieking goblins.

Nessa's jaw dropped as she surveyed the scene.

"Stay back," yelled Demelza, "we're overrun! We'll come to you!"

HISSSSSSS! Captain Honkers spat as a snot goblin scampered up behind him and tried to pull a feather from his tail.

"Hands off my goose!" yelled Demelza, slapping away the goblin's grimy grasping hands with a foam sword. More goblins started to gather, grabbing excitedly at her swords and Game Gauntlet as they wailed and screeched, drool running down their chins:

"Me!"

"Mine!"

"Gimme!"

"Me want! Me want now!"

Demelza fought hard, but it was no use, there were too many of them. Captain Honkers took to the air, squawking as the horde closed in. Demelza raised her face to the sky and screamed up at him: "It's too late for me, Honkers. Save yourself! Say goodbye to Nessa for me!"

Then darkness closed in. She fell to the floor, holding on to her swords with all her might as the goblins tried to tear them from her grasp. There was no point in fighting it. The caravan park belonged to the horde now. Just as her swords and gauntlet began to slip from her fingers, she heard a muffled battle cry over the din.

"Pennnn-furrrr-zeeeeee Kniiiiiights foreverrrrr!"

Daylight broke through. A hand reached down and grasped Demelza's arm. Demelza shaded her eyes from the morning sun to see a face beaming down at her as the goblins scattered.

"Need a ride?" Nessa asked.

Demelza leapt onto the back of Neon Justice whooping with glee. She waved her battered swords, laughing as the goblins ran from Neon Justice. Honkers flew over them honking loudly as they rode victoriously through the park gates and freewheeled down the hill towards town.

Demelza closed her eyes and tilted her head back so the sun warmed her cheeks as she breathed in the fresh smell of spring on the breeze.

"Thanks for the rescue," she said, wrapping her arms around Nessa's waist and giving her a big squeezy hug. "I thought the snot goblins had got us good!"

Nessa laughed as they slowed for the bend at the bottom of the hill and rolled over a little wooden bridge.

"You were a snot goblin once, D. We all were. And my Dad said the tourists are bringing in a lot of money, he's even meeting your dad this afternoon to talk about extending the park and buying more caravans."

"MORE caravans?" shouted Demelza, clenching her fist and waving her Game Gauntlet at the sky. "So that more noisy, nosy, smelly tourists can mess up MY caravan park?"

"Don't forget, the tourists are the reason you still have a caravan park," said Nessa, as they swerved to avoid a couple of kids more interested in their ice-creams than looking where they were going. "And if your Dad and my parents are working hard to bring in tourists, maaaaabye you could be a teeny-tiny bit friendlier to their kids?"

Demelza picked a little scab off her chin and flicked it over her shoulder. Maybe Nessa was right.

"I'll think about it," she said with a nod. "But first, let's go to the arcade. They've fixed the Luxulyan Warriors machine. I bet I can beat your high score this time!"

"You're on!" Nessa hit her horn to warn off the seagulls as they took a shortcut down an alley full of lobster pots. "Maybe you'll be fifty-sixth time lucky…"

Chapter Two
CONVOY!

"Twenty-nine thousand nine hundred and ninety!" shouted Demelza as she hammered the buttons of the blooping arcade machine. "Thirty thousand. Yes! Extra life! I'm coming for your score, Nessa!"

"Nice going, D," said Nessa resting her chin on Demelza's shoulder, "just another twenty-one thousand, five hundred and sixty points to go. Watch out for that…"

"What?" shouted Demelza, pummelling the wallop button as a character in a horned helmet ran onto the screen behind her.

"…berserker."

"Nooo!" Demelza wailed as the berserker bopped her character on the head. Her warrior's eyes turned to little crosses and the machine let out a loud ***bleep-bleep-bleeep-bleeeeep-blooop, spadoi-oi-oing!***

"Thirty-eight thousand five hundred. Your best yet," said Nessa, gently punching her arm. "You'll beat me next time."

"I would have beat you there," grumbled Demelza as she spelled out D-E-M on the high score table under the letters N-E-S which filled the first two lines of the highest ever scores. "Only you was breathing too loud in my ear and distracting me."

"My bad," said Nessa with a straight face, "I won't move, talk, breathe or exist next time. Then you'll totally beat my score."

Demelza looked at her sideways. Nessa's face was completely straight with only the tiniest twinkle in her eye.

"Hmm, well, yes. Good," she lifted Captain Honkers down from his perch on top of the arcade cabinet. "Now, seeing as you made me lose, you can buy me an ice-cream."

"Sure," Nessa grinned as they left the bleepy-bloopy music and noises of the arcade and hopped back on Neon Justice.

"With a flake, an' sprinkles, an' a big squirt of beetle blood."

"You got it."

There was a long queue at the ice cream van, but it was worth it once they were sitting on the pier, legs dangling over the edge as they ate their ice-creams, slurping up the drips and raspberry sauce that dribbled down over their hands. Captain Honkers pattered around behind them, happily snapping up pieces of wafer. A deep horn sounded as the Penfurzy ferry pulled into the harbour.

"More invaders," grumbled Demelza, licking her hands clean and running her tongue around the outside of her mouth as cars started to roll off the ferry.

"OK, holiday makers!" She corrected herself as Nessa raised an eyebrow. "With lots of lovely money to spend at the caravan park and golf course."

"Better," Nessa nodded. "Whoa, look at that!"

A row of brightly coloured lorries and caravans were driving off the ferry. They tooted their horns as they headed through town in a convoy.

"It's a fair!" Demelza squealed, "the fair has come back to Penfurzy!" She drummed her fists on the railing then jumped up to wave at the trucks as they carried their strange cargo of dismantled rides painted with quirky images of popular cartoon characters. "It's a fair, Nessa. A FAIR!"

"I can see that," said Nessa, "cool. I haven't been on a ferris wheel or dodgems since before we moved here."

Demelza stared at her, eyes wide.

"You... you've been to a fair before?"

"Of course," said Nessa. "One used to come to town twice a year when I lived on the mainland. It was a pretty cool place to hang out. What's the big deal?"

"The big deal?" Demelza shook her head as if trying to shake some sense into Nessa's words. "The big deal is that I've NEVER been to a fair before! The last time this one came to Penfurzy was ten years ago, before I was even born. The closest I've ever been to dodgems are the old rusty ones in Madern Stibb's scrapyard."

"You've never been to a fair?" asked Nessa in surprise. "Never-ever?"

"Never-ever-ever!" said Demelza. Her stomach felt fluttery with excitement. She grasped Nessa's arms and danced her around in circles. Captain Honkers ran around them flapping his wings and honking excitedly as Demelza sang:

"We're going to the fair-air, we're going to the fair-air!" Nessa tried to stay cool but finally gave in and snorted with laughter as she joined in the silly song.

"We're going to the fair-air, we're going to win a goldfish, we're going to ride the waltzers, and scream until we're SICK!"

"Arr, I wouldn't be celebrating the arrival of that lot," said a cracked voice from a bench behind them.

"Mister Greensplat?" said Demelza, as they turned to see a bearded old man in oilskins climbing out of a fishing boat with a bucket of pollock. "What's wrong with the fair? Mum and Dad always told me it's the bestest ever, even if it only comes to Penfurzy every ten years."

"That be ten years too often," grumbled the old man. He refilled his pipe and glared at the tooting trucks from under his huge bushy brows. "They're a funny lot, those fair folk. They bring bad luck with them. My one true love left me forever when they was here sixty years ago. Said goodbye to me while we was riding the ferris wheel. I had a ring in my pocket ready to give her that night, but it was the last time I ever saw her. She left and never came back. She could have been Mrs Greensplat.'

'Lucky lady,' grinned Nessa.

'Mark my words, there's strange   goings on whenever they comes to Penfurzy."

"Yeah, but there's always strange goings on in Penfurzy," said Nessa. "Ancient curses, castles rising from the sea, pipe smoking old salts giving mysterious warnings…"

"Cheek!" he grumbled, as he lit his pipe and let out a puff of smoke that made him look like a grumpy old dragon. "Penfurzy might have its oddities, but that's good old homegrown strange stuff. We don't wants no fair folk bringing their own strange stuff over to our island!"

"What kind of strange stuff?" asked Demelza. Her skin tingled. It had been nearly five months since their last big adventure, though Nessa helped make sure they had at least a mini adventure every week. Her nose was itching to sniff out another good mystery.

"Merrin Carnkie thinks they're up to something at the old quarry. They always set up near there. She sez every time they're here they go tramping down into the quarry at night and don't come out until morning. Sez all these strange noises come echoing out of the rabbit holes on the tor."

"What sort of noises?" whispered Demelza.

"Pfht! Probably the voices in Merrin's own head," he wheezed, "no, I'll tells you what they're up to…" he beckoned them towards him. Demelza and Nessa moved in closer. He looked from side to side then hissed;

"Pie."

"Pie?" repeated Nessa.

"Pie! They's after stealin' the recipe for my stargazy pie. Ooh, hello Mr Greensplat, they sez. Can we order a dozen of your delicious stargazy pies? If you ever want to share the recipe we'll gladly pay you for it. Best pie in the world is that. Well they're right, my pies are the best in the world, but they're not taking my grandpa's recipe off this island. That's Penfurzy pie. Penfurzy is where it's staying!"

Demelza jumped as a loud horn tooted. A tall man with a ponytail, tanned muscly arms and a faded black skull t-shirt leaned out of his lorry window and shouted:

"Morning, Mr Greensplat! Good to see you again. I'll send my son Jack down with our usual order for your delicious pies."

"I'll get the oven on now!" the old fisherman called back with a wave. "See what I mean," he growled to the girls, "pie! They'll have run out of cats for makin' those hotdogs they sell, so I bets they're wantin' to sell my pies. Well, they can come back all they like, but they'll never find out that my secret ingredients are a pinch of nutmeg, a couple of cloves and a small grating of…" His pipe dropped to the floor as he clamped his hand over his mouth. "Spies!" he shouted as he grabbed his bucket of fish.

"Tell them it was a nice try, but there's no way they're getting their hands on that recipe, or my name isn't Humfra Meriasek Greensplat!"

Nessa looked at Demelza and shook her head as they watched him scurry down the pier, pausing briefly to yell back to Demelza, "Tell yer dad I said hi!"

"Will do. Byyyye, Mr Greensplat," Demelza shouted as he hurried home. "He's a bit odd," she whispered to Nessa. "Tells everyone he used to go out with a mermaid."

"Each to their own," said Nessa. "The fair is setting up by the quarry, eh?" She grabbed onto her bike. "What are we waiting for? Let's go get your bike and get over there!"

Chapter Three
ROGUE AVENGER

It was early afternoon by the time Demelza, Nessa and Captain Honkers crested the hill that led down to the quarry and nearby fields.

"Whoa!" gasped Demelza. She squeezed the brakes on her bike and stared down to where the lorries had formed a huge semicircle in a field in the shadow of the tor. An army of people were unloading machinery and huge panels painted with rockets, sports cars, cartoon characters and film stars.

"Look, Nessa!" Demelza bounced on her seat. "They've got a ferris wheel, and a Helter

Skelter! Ooh! What's the Matterhorn? And Stratorockets? Plummeting Paratroopers? A Meteorite Cage. Aaaaaargh, I want to go on ALL of them!"

"Chill your boots!" said Nessa, "We will. Careful on The Meteorite though. A kid at my old school went on that one after eating three hotdogs, an ice-cream and a bag of candy floss, and then got really sick on the ride. It span so fast that the puke hit everyone on it. Every. Single. Person. Right in the face. Then they started puking too. The puke began flying out of the ride and hitting people walking by, then they started puking. The fairground had to be closed for two days and you could still smell the puke when it reopened."

"Coooool!" said Demelza, eyes wide. "Come on, let's go see if they need any help setting up."

Captain Honkers had already flown ahead and was flapping from lorry to lorry watching the hustle and bustle, while keeping an eye out for any tasty treats that might happen to drop from the interesting snack stands that were being set up.

"It even smeeells exciting," said Demelza, sniffing the air to take in the scent of axle grease, crushed grass, canvas and whatever was cooking in the tents being set up behind the lorries.

"Oh, man! what's that?" said Nessa. A strange device, like two giant gramophone horns joined together by the narrow ends, sat in the fair's campground. The wide mouth at one end lay flat on the ground, and the other pointed at the tents.

Honk?

Demelza took her head out of the horn.

"Oh, no. Get out of there, Honkers!" she ran after the goose as he waddled into a tent. There was a yell, a clatter of pots and pans and a lot of honking.

"Naughty Honkers!" Demelza waved her finger at him as he flapped back out, chased by a boy around Nessa's age. He was tall and wiry with a twisted afro held back from his freckled face with a fabric band. He wore a silver feather earring in one ear, knee-length bleach-washed jeans, a studded belt and a vest with a tiger on it.

"Rad vest," said Nessa with a nod.

"Sorry about Honkers," Demelza picked the goose up under her arm. "He's just excited. It's the first time he's seen a fair. Me too, actually."

"No harm done," said the boy, "Though he made me drop a sack of spuds all over the floor when he came honking up behind me, and he didn't half give Ellie a fright."

"Is Ellie your sister?" asked Demelza.

"Nope," said the boy as the biggest goose Demelza had ever seen burst out of the tent, stretched herself tall, flapped her wings and honked angrily. Captain Honkers tucked his head into Demelza's armpit in terror.

"Chill, Ellie," said the boy. "That's enough. He's learnt his lesson." He stroked her neck with the back of his fingers. The goose kept her eyes fixed on Captain Honkers. "This is Aurelian. Ellie for short. She doesn't stand for any nonsense."

"Hear that, Honkers?" said Demelza sternly. "Behave yourself."

"I'd better get back to the tatties," said Jack. "Dad wants me to peel the lot and chop them into chips for when we open tomorrow."

"We'll give you a hand," said Nessa with a shrug. Peeling potatoes wasn't exactly how Demelza had imagined helping out (she thought she'd have been better at assembling the ferris wheel), but the boy was wearing a tiger vest and looked as though he might have some cool stories to tell.

An hour later they were sitting ankle deep in potato peel. Ellie was settled in a large dog basket casting stern glances at Captain Honkers whenever he started snooping around the tent for snacks. Jack was talking about all the places the fair had visited recently. He tilted his head to one side and squinted at Nessa.

"You know you look a lot like this kid who puked over everyone on The Meteorite ride last time we visited…"

"SO, YOU SAID YOUR DAD WAS BORN IN PENFURZY?" Nessa interrupted, very loudly. Demelza couldn't help noticing that her brown cheeks looked flushed. "But you haven't been since the last time the fair was here?"

"Nope," said Jack, "And I was only two years old then. You guys will have to give me the tour when we're not so busy. I bet you know all the best places to see."

"Oh, we do!" said Demelza, "There's the castle what me an' Nessa discovered last year, and the crazy golf course up at the caravan park my dad owns… with Nessa's parents," she added quickly. "They own a bit of it too. But me an' Dad are the ones that live there."

"Then there's Saffron Records. Karensa works there," Nessa sighed, "she's cool. Flyer than an actual fly. Oh, and the arcade is pretty sweet, they've got Robotronic, Super Viper, Operation Wolverine, and Luxulyan Warriors."

"Nessa's king of that game," said Demelza proudly, "no-one has ever beaten her score, not even me. It's impossible!"

"Is that so?" said Jack, one eyebrow raised.

"Many have tried, many have failed," said Nessa, throwing back her shoulders and lifting her chin proudly.

Demelza stopped halfway through peeling a potato. A beautiful sound had drifted into the tent. It wrapped around them like a soft, warm blanket. Someone was singing. No, singing wasn't a good enough word for the sound. It made Demelza feel as though an angel had kissed her forehead and told her that every day of her life would be as filled with magic as the first day of the summer holidays.

Honk! said Captain Honkers, pattering outside to investigate.

Honk-honk! Ellie charged after him and nipped angrily at his tail feathers.

Nessa dropped her peeler and followed the geese outside.

"Wait!" shouted Jack, running after Demelza as she dashed after Nessa. The voice was coming from a caravan decorated with swirling colours, shells and smooth pieces of seaglass. A pale woman with long reddish blonde hair was sitting by the window. Her head rested on her hands as she sang to the gulls and puffins flying overhead. Demelza and Nessa stood spellbound. They didn't understand the words, but somehow they could feel that she was talking to the birds, the sky, the sea and the land, like an old friend returning. Captain Honkers sat silently, eyes closed, beak lifted to the sky as he listened. Even Ellie didn't seem so angry to have another goose invading her campsite as the beautiful song came to an end.

"That, was beeee-yew-tee-ful!" sighed Demelza.

The woman smiled down at them.

"Thank you," her voice was soft and lilting with a slight Penfurzy accent, "it's an old, old song. The gulls made me think of it. My grandmother taught it to me, her grandmother taught her. There are many songs passed down through my family. I'm the only one who remembers them all now, and I'm afraid some have been lost."

"Well you sing it reeeelly good. What's your name? I'm Demelza Penrose. This is my best friend, Nessa, and this is Captain Honkers, the honkiest goose in the whole wide world. Say hello to the nice lady, Honkers."

HONK!

"I'm Morvoren," the woman's blue-green eyes twinkled and her hair swung forwards as she leaned down to shake their hands. "You can call me Ren. Lovely to meet you."

"Are you from round here?" asked Nessa.

"What are you guys, the Spanish Inquisition?" asked Jack, pushing between them. "Sorry for these nosy parkers, Ren. Come on you two. Back in the tent before I get into…"

"Jack! What's going on here?" bellowed a voice.

"Too late," sighed Jack. The man who had called out from his lorry to order pies from Mr Greensplat was storming towards them. He didn't look happy. Morvoren ducked back into her caravan and closed the window.

"Who are those girls? You know the public can't come back here. You know why! And why is Ellie out? JACK! You know better than this!"

"Sorry, Dad," Jack stepped in front of Nessa and Demelza. "They weren't snooping or anything. They were helping me out and heard Ren singing."

"It was lovely!" said Demelza, "you should sell tickets for people to hear her. I bet you'd sell loads and loads and loads. We'll tell everyone in town how good she is."

"We could even sell tickets for you," said Nessa.

"No, no, NO!" snapped Jack's dad, "Don't you tell anyone about her. Jack, this is exactly why we don't let people back here. Remember Japan?"

"I know, Dad. But Nessa and Demelza are cool. They…"

Boom! BOOM! BOOM!

Jack stumbled and knocked Demelza into Nessa as a terrifying noise blared out of the weird horn device. Captain Honkers took to the sky and honked down at them as the half-built fairground rides rattled and shook. Ellie hissed and flapped off into Morvoren's caravan.

"Earthquake!" Nessa dragged Demelza to her feet and they ran for their bikes.

"Get them out of here, Jack!" shouted his dad as he went to help the other fair folk secure the equipment. **"NOW!"**

Chapter Four
IT LIVES!

The noise and tremors had stopped by the time the girls had cycled full pelt out of the fairground gates, but they kept on riding, down the road and all the way up the steep hill. When they reached the disused train tracks they dropped their bikes, and flopped down, rubbing their aching legs as they caught their breath.

"Honkers! It's OK, we're safe!" Demelza shouted up to the goose. He swooped down into her arms and buried his head in her frizzy curls.

"How weird was that?" panted Nessa. "Has there ever been an earthquake on Penfurzy before?"

"Hmmm I can't remember one," Demelza rubbed her nose, "oh, wait! Dad told me the quarry was shut down about fifty years ago, a few months after it opened, because the mining was causing tremors.

And I remember Mum said there were a couple of little ones when I was in her tum. She saw the ripples on the boating lake while she was feeding the swans."

"A little bit before you were born?" Nessa rubbed her chin. So, about ten years ago?"

"Must have been," said Demelza, "…yes! Because she said they'd just been to the fair when it happened."

"So, the last time the fair was here was also the last time it happened? Innnnnteresting."

"Ooooh, do you think there's a mystery to solve?" Demelza dropped Captain Honkers and clapped her hands.

"I'm not sure,' said Nessa, "but old Greensplat is right. There's something funny about the fair, and that horn thing. I wonder if that's what caused it?"

"Well, if anyone can find out," said Demelza, "It's…"

"The Penfurzy Rebel Bicycle Club!" they both shouted. They spat in their palms and launched into their secret club handshake, while Captain Honkers circled them honking excitedly.

"Wait up!" came a distant shout. Jack was pedalling up the hill on a very squeaky bike. Its frame was so rusted that Demelza expected it to fall apart underneath him at any moment. "Sorry about Dad," he panted as he finally reached the top and dropped down beside them. "It's just we had a bit of bother somewhere we visited a few months ago."

"Japan?" said Demelza. "Nessa has been there. Tell him about when you trained with ninjas, Nessa." Nessa gave her a quick jab with her elbow. "Ow! What was that for?" Demelza rubbed her arm. Nessa usually jumped on any chance to tell one of her amazing stories, although... Demelza realised she hadn't told any recently.

"What happened in Japan that got your dad's knickers in a knot?" asked Nessa.

Jack bit his lip. He glanced over his shoulder then back at the girls. "He'd go mad if he knew I was talking about it."

"We can keep secrets," said Demelza, "We haven't told anyone that Mr Calenick, who works in our caravan park, is really a headless..."

"Cough-cough!" said Nessa very loudly, giving Demelza another nudge. "We can keep our lips zipped," she told him.

"Promise?" said Jack.

"Promise," said Demelza.

Honk! said Captain Honkers.

"Cross your hearts and hope to die?"

The girls drew crosses across their hearts, clutched their hands to their throats and rolled their eyes back into their heads.

"Stick a needle in your eye?"

They pretended to pop their eyeballs and sprayed invisible eye-jelly over Jack. He gave an approving nod and lowered his voice.

"Someone tried to kidnap Ren."

"Whoa, who would try to kidnap her?" asked Nessa.

"We still don't know," said Jack, "but while we were loading up to leave, a lorry, just like one of ours, turned up and loaded her caravan in the back. It happened so quickly we didn't realise what was going on until they were driving away. Dad was the only person to act. He grabbed a rock for his catapult, fired it at the lorry and smashed off the lock. Good job they were in too much of a rush to tie the caravan down, it rolled out the back. Smashed up the wheels pretty bad but saved Ren. If Dad wasn't such a crack shot with a catapult she'd have been gone. Forever. At least they didn't know about Ellie too."

"What about Ellie?" asked Nessa.

"Oh, you know, she's gigantic. Probably a world record."

"Why did they want to kidnap Ren?" asked Demelza. "'Cos of her singing?"

"Partly," said Jack, "She… well, Ren's special, really important. We need to keep her safe."

"Is she related to you?" asked Nessa.

"No, but our families have been really close for generations. I've known Ren all my life. She's been travelling with the fair for over fifty, er, I mean, twenty years now."

Nessa's eyes narrowed. She opened her mouth to ask another question but Jack held up his hands.

"Can we leave it now. Please? What happened was because someone blabbed too much to strangers, just like I'm doing now."

"We're not strange," said Demelza, giving her widest grin. "And we won't blab about Ren."

"Not that you actually told us much anyway," said Nessa.

"Good enough," Jack hopped back on his bike, "OK, we've done enough chips. Dad's still annoyed so Mum said I can clear off for the afternoon. How's about you guys show me around?"

"Let's head to mine," said Nessa. "Dad's up at the caravan park and Mum's out on coastguard duty, so the garage will be free for surgery."

"Surgery?" Jack leaned away, one eyebrow raised. "I was thinking we could head to the arcade."

"First things first," said Nessa, "if you're going to be seen riding with us, we've GOT to do something about that bike!"

Back in the old garage behind the converted windmill where Nessa lived with her mum and dad, Nessa leaned over Jack's bike in goggles and a face mask. She let out a long whistle as she examined the frame and held out her gloved hand to Demelza.

"Oil!"

"Oil." Demelza said as she handed her a can of machine oil. Nessa dripped some onto the bike chain and axles then turned the pedals until the squeaking stopped and a smooth clicking was heard.

"Rag!" said Nessa.

"Rag." Demelza slapped a cloth into Nessa's outstretched hand.

"Rust-Buster!" said Nessa.

"Rust-Buster." Demelza pulled on her own facemask and carefully poured liquid from a red bottle onto the cloth.

"What are you doing to my bike?" asked Jack, leaning over their shoulders as they worked.

"Shh!" Demelza moved him back with one hand as the other mopped Nessa's brow with a clean cloth. "Don't distract her. This is where we'll find out."

"Find out what?"

"If she'll pull through," Demelza handed Nessa another soaked rag and crossed her fingers tightly as Nessa ran it carefully and thoroughly over the sanded frame, stripping off the remaining rust until the stained but rust-free metal frame was finally revealed.

At last, Nessa stepped back. She tossed the rag into a bucket, pulled down her mask and let out a long breath. She gave Demelza a nod.

"No holes. She's sound."

"Yes!" Demelza punched the air then grasped Jack by the arms. "Did you hear that, Jack? Did you hear it? She's going to make it. She's **ALIIIIIVE!**"

"Ready for phase two?" Nessa leaned back to press play on her boombox. A fast, funky tune blared out as she shook a spray can in each hand.

"Ready!" Demelza threw Jack a face mask. "Let's get to work!"

Captain Honkers kept his eyes fixed firmly on the shed as he stood outside and marched on the spot, stomping the ground with his webbed feet and gobbling up every worm that wriggled out of the mud to see if it was raining. The sawing, scratching and clicking noises had stopped and something was rattling and hissing in there. When he was finally too full to gobble up another worm, he waddled over for a closer look.

HONK! he squawked as the doors burst open. Out strode Demelza, Nessa and Jack, wheeling a shiny, multi-coloured bike. It had a tin tray shield tied to the front and a tiger flag, that looked roughly vest shaped, flying from the back.

"It's amazing!" said Jack when he finally found his voice. "Thank you. I've never had anything this cool in my whole life."

"Dude, you live in a fairground," said Nessa.

"It's not as rad as you think," said Jack. "Mum and Dad have money but they don't believe in flashy stuff. Everything I have is shared or second hand. This is one hundred percent mine, and one thousand percent awesome!" He held up his hand and Nessa and Demelza high-fived him together.

"Now you just need to name her," said Demelza, "We can help with that." She pulled a folded piece of paper out of her pocket and carefully unfolded it as if it was very, very precious. It was held together with sticky tape. "This is a very science-tific way of naming steeds. Me an' Nessa made it last half-term holiday."

"OK, first letter of your first name is J," said Nessa scanning the page. "And you have…" she squinted at him, "Sort of greeny-grey-blue eyes. Let's just say blue 'cos that works best."

"Best for what?" asked Jack. "What does my eye colour have to do with anything?"

"Shh!" Demelza made a tick on the page with a pencil stub she found in her hair. "Next, we need the last letter of your last name."

"I don't have one."

Demelza and Nessa stared at him.

"No, really. What's your last name?" said Nessa.

"I'm just Jack. So is my dad, so was his dad, and his dad, as long as anyone can remember."

Nessa sniffed the air and squinted at Jack.

"Seriously?"

"Scouts honour," said Jack.

"That's not the scout salute," said Nessa as he held up two fingers in the sign of peace, "but OK, Just Jack. I guess we'll use the last letter of your first name instead."

"K," Demelza stuck her tongue out of the side of her mouth as she scrolled down the page, "last question, are you right or left-handed?"

"Left," said Jack, "But why…?"

"Shooooooooosh!" yelled Demelza. "This is important workin's out! J, blue eyes, K, left-handed. Got it!" she made another tick and showed Nessa the page. "Your official bike name is…"

Nessa rolled her tongue and slapped her hands on her jeans to create a drumroll to build up the tension.

"Rogue Avenger!" Demelza punched her fist into the air. "May she live long and serve you well."

"Rogue Avenger," Nessa raised her own fist.

"Rogue Avenger," Jack joined the salute with a smile. "Perfect."

Thanks to a bag of ten pence coins Nessa's mum had left for them, by the time the sun hung low in the sky, the gang had played every single machine at the bustling arcade, even the toy grabber that no-one ever-ever-ever managed to get a prize from.

"I can't believe you won," said Demelza as a teddy bear dropped down the chute and into Jack's waiting hands. "Nessa says those machines are all rigged."

"They are," said Jack. "You've just got to watch the machine and time it right. It only grips properly once a set number of people lose. Here," he thrust the teddy at them. "For you guys."

Demelza looked at the cuddly toy in her hands. Nessa rolled her eyes.

"A teddy? You think just 'cos we're girls we like teddies, dollies and big fluffy unicorns?"

"I LOVE it!" Demelza hugged the bear so hard his eyes bulged and his belly popped a stitch. Nessa buried her face in her palm but couldn't help smiling.

"Tomorrow is opening night," said Jack, as Demelza tied the teddy into the pride of place at the front of her bike. "Come find me. I'll make sure you never have to pay for a ride."

He waved all the way down the street as he cycled proudly home on Rogue Avenger, dodging the clusters of tourists around all the little souvenir shops.

"Free rides!" said Demelza. "My favourite kind of rides!"

Nessa was quiet.

"Everything OK?" Demelza asked as they cycled back to the caravan park.

"Yeah. There's just something a bit funny about him, don't you think?"

"Jack? No way. He's the coolest," said Demelza. How could anyone think anything else about a kid who lived on a fairground with a giant goose and a dad who had a catapult? "Ohhh, he beat your high score. Don't worry. I bet it was beginner's luck. You'll be in the top spot again in no time!"

"It's not that," said Nessa. "It's that whole fairground. I mean, there are only earth tremors when they're here. What if they're causing them with that weird machine? And Jack's dad, what's his deal? He reeeeally didn't want us talking to Ren. What if he's keeping her locked up, and those people in Japan were trying to rescue her?"

"No way, José!" said Demelza as they pedalled up the hill.

"What makes you so sure?" said Nessa.

"Cos she's standing right there." Demelza pointed up the clifftop path. Ren was standing in the twilight, eyes closed, face turned into the cool, salty breeze blowing in from the sea.

"She's a bit close," said Nessa. "What's she doing?"

Demelza didn't answer. She couldn't. Her whole body had frozen. Her heart had stopped beating. What was Ren doing so close to the edge? These were the same cliffs her own mother had fallen from. What if Ren… She tried to find enough breath to shout a warning but her lungs were empty. All she could do was stare and let out a strangled cry as Ren took a running jump and launched herself off the cliff, plummeting into the cold, dark water far, far below without a sound.

Chapter Five
THE LIE

Demelza shivered on the battered sofa in her kitchen, despite the roaring fire and the warmth of Nessa and her dad sitting on either side of her. Her dad wrapped one of his big strong arms around her as she leaned into his shoulder. Constable Dobwalls was standing by the door on his walkie-talkie, his face grim.

"OK. Let me know when you find something," he clipped the walkie-talkie to his uniform and sat down opposite them. "We have four boats searching the harbour and volunteers searching the beaches. Two officers are on their way up to the fairground."

Demelza couldn't help but imagine Jack's face when he heard what had happened. She remembered how she had felt when she heard about her mum's accident. It was as if the floor had vanished under her and she was endlessly falling, even while her dad had hugged her tight, one of his shirt buttons pressed against her nose as his own shoulders shook.

A bright light cast moving shadows onto the ceiling as the headlights of a car shone through the window as it pulled up. Nessa grabbed her bag.

"That's Dad," said Nessa. "Mum will be out in her boat leading the search party. I'd better go, but I'll call you if I hear anything." She gave Demelza a long, silent hug. Neither of them said anything, but each knew how the other felt.

"I'll walk you out," said Constable Dobwalls.

A hot tear ran down Demelza's cheek as Nessa left. It dripped off her chin onto her dungarees. She wiped it away with her sleeve as she stared out of the window and watched Nessa hug her dad then get into the back of the car as the constable spoke to her dad.

"You're thinking about her, aren't you?" said her dad.

"You mean Mum?" Demelza nodded. He gave her another squeeze and a little sob escaped her.

"I think about her every day," said Demelza. "Good things," she added quickly, "not the way she… you know."

44

"I know," said her dad. "I do too."

"You do?" Demelza blinked up at him. They didn't talk about her mum much. She sometimes wondered if her dad was forgetting her.

"Of course. I think about how her favourite ice-cream was banana choc chip, but she didn't like the taste of real bananas. I think about how much she liked to draw and paint, how happy and beautiful she looked the day you were born, how she was always looking for new adventures and wrote down every mystery she found in her notebooks. She said one day you might solve them if she couldn't." He kissed her forehead and smiled. "And she was right, you've started solving them already. She'd be so proud."

"She wrote those down… for me?" sniffed Demelza.

"Some before you were even born. She was taking you on adventures with us when you were in her tummy, searching for piskies, spriggans and mermaids. One day, when you were very nearly ready to be born, she took me to the quarry, and then the harbour, to search for tunnels to a giant cavern below Penfurzy. She'd heard about it in an ancient legend. We never found it, but we enjoyed the adventure." He pinched the corners of his eyes with his forefinger and thumb. Demelza wrapped her arms around him and held on tight.

"We've both been feeling sad and missing her on our own, Dad.
But when we miss her together, it doesn't feel as sad."

"Then we'll miss her together more often," he kissed the top
of her head again. "Now, let's feed the geese, then it's bath and
bedtime."

Knock-knock-knock

Demelza jumped as Constable Dobwalls knocked on the window
again. He was on his walkie-talkie again. He hurried round to the
door.

"Thanks. Keep the team searching for another hour and
report back. Over," he scratched his head and sat down
opposite Demelza.

"You're absolutely sure it was this woman, Morvoren, from the
fair that you saw?"

Demelza nodded.

"Have they… have they found her?" asked her dad.

The constable nodded.

"They found her."

Demelza clapped her hand to her mouth.

"Is she…" she couldn't finish the sentence.

"She's at home. At the fair. In her caravan."

"At the fair?" Demelza's mind whirled. How could she be
back there?

"Said she hadn't left her caravan all day. The boy you said we should talk to…" the constable checked his notebook, "Jack. He confirmed she hadn't left."

Demelza shook her head. It was Ren they had seen. Why would Jack lie too?"

"They're fibbing," she said, "Jack was with us all afternoon. He couldn't know if she'd left or not. Nessa saw her too. She just ran and jumped off the cliff with a smile on her face. Whoever they saw in her caravan, it wasn't Ren!"

The constable tucked the notebook in his pocket and knelt down to speak to Demelza eye to eye. "I'm not saying you're telling fibs…" he said gently.

"Good! Cos I'm not!" said Demelza.

"But… are you sure about what you saw? Remember when you girls messed up Madern Stibb's scrapyard and told me a giant iron knight had come to life and smashed the place up?"

"It did! It was…" Demelza stopped as the constable gave her an annoying, understanding smile.

"Maybe your imagination and, well, what happened to your mum made you think you saw something, or someone, who wasn't really there."

Demelza opened her mouth to argue but felt her dad's hand on her shoulder. The constable had made up his mind. She knew what happened when adults made up their minds. The thought got carved into stone in their brains and couldn't ever be changed. "I'll ask Nessa's mum to keep her team searching the harbour, but nothing has been found so far and no one has been reported missing." He smiled at Demelza again. "That's good news, isn't it?"

Demelza bit her lip and nodded. She grabbed a bucket and stomped off with Captain Honkers to feed the rest of the geese.

"It was Ren," she muttered as she scattered grain. "I saw her, Nessa saw her, and so did you, Honkers."

Honk! agreed Captain Honkers, as she fished a juicy worm out of her pocket for him.

"She can't be back at the fair. Jack is lying. Me, you, an' Nessa, we're going to find out why!"

Chapter Six
LAST CARRIAGE TO HELL

Demelza's stomach did a little flip as the crowded bus she was sitting on with Nessa and Captain Honkers crawled over the brow of the hill. They were at the north end of the island and saw the fair spread out in the field below. It was half past four in the afternoon and the sun hung low in the sky. The colourful lights of the rides gave a magical glow to the fairground. All thoughts of confronting Jack disappeared for a moment as Demelza stared in awe at the colourful tents and the spinning, swinging, bobbing and whirling rides, each blaring out its own tune.

"We'll
do that one first!"
Nessa pointed at the towering
Helter Skelter slide. "It's good to start with if
you haven't been to a fair before. We'll be able to
see the whole fairground and decide what to go on
next. And we should get hotdogs and eat them on the
Ferris Wheel."

"Ooh, and candyfloss," said Demelza, "and
cherry slushies!" Her Dad had given her four
whole pounds and she could feel them burning
a hole in her pocket. She hugged Captain
Honkers, who was sitting surprisingly well-
behaved on her knee.

"Um, maybe take it easy, you don't want
to puke on everyone else on the ride," said
Nessa, her cheeks a little pink again. They
got up and made their way to the front of the
bus as it reached the bottom of the hill.

"Personally, I'd like to see just how ghostly
that ghost train really is," said a voice from
Nessa's backpack.

"Shh!" Nessa hissed over her shoulder as the pickled knight's watery blue eyes peered out at Demelza through two holes cut into the fabric.

"Why didn't you bring your body?" asked Demelza, "then you could have walked around on your own and talked to people, instead of being stuck in there."

"I left it tidying the shed," said the pickled knight. "I never thought I'd say this, but bodies, well, they're overrated. All their functions and noises, aches and pains, ugh! It's good to take a break from it all now and again. Besides, this is like old times, The Penfurzy Rebel Bicycle Club, together again!"

"Ok," said Nessa. "But keep schtum whenever there's anyone in earshot, agreed? People get worried when they hear a talking bag."

"They'd be even more worried to see a talking head," grinned Demelza.

They hopped off the bus at the bottom of the hill and raced the crowd through the gates and into a full-blown riot of colours, sounds and smells.

"Mmm, toffee apples!" said Demelza, sniffing deeply, "and candy floss, and popcorn, and hot dogs!" Her stomach let out a noise like a whimpering dog. "There-there," she said, giving it a pat. "Soooon! I'll feed you soon."

"We've got twelve pounds between us," said Nessa. "If your dad's picking us up at half past seven, then we've got three whole hours here, that's four pounds to spend per hour."

"We're RICH!" shouted Demelza.

"Shhh and come on…" she grabbed Demelza's hand. "I bet we can see where Jack is from the Helter Skelter. We know what we saw the other day, and he's going to tell us why they're covering it up!"

It seemed everyone on Penfurzy was at the fair on opening night. They had to queue for ten minutes just for the Helter Skelter. Captain Honkers was already at the top of the slide honking, as he waited for them to climb the spiral steps.

"Any sign of Jack?" asked Demelza, peering out of each little window on the way up.

"Nope," said Nessa, "maybe he's not working tonight?"

"Or maybe he didn't want to run into us," said Demelza, scanning the fair from the top of the slide.

"Oi! Red! Mini-goth!" yelled the woman they had paid at the entrance. "Get a move on, there's a queue!"

"Goth? I'm not a goth," Nessa made a fist with her fingerless leather glove. "What is it with people and labels? Goth! If anything, I'm more a…"

"Nessa!" Demelza dropped her straw mat down at the top of the slide and yelled, "last one to the bottom is a rotten egg!" She jumped onto the mat, wrapped her hands through the loops on the sides and pushed off.

"Wheeeeeee!"

The mat whizzed down and down, and around and around.

"Whooooooo!"

She felt as though she had left her stomach at the top of the slide as her anorak cape flapped behind her.

HOOOOOOOOONK! honked Captain Honkers,

swooping around the tower to keep up with her.

"Wah-hoooo!" she heard Nessa yell from far behind her, with a more muffled "Yaaaaaaargh!" from the pickled knight in her backpack.

"That," screamed Demelza as her mat whizzed off the slide and across the crash pad at the bottom, "was… Brill-ee-ANT!" She rolled out of the way as Nessa came shooting out behind her. "Let's do it again, race you to the top!"

"One more time," said Nessa. "Then, the BIG stuff!"

Two hours later Demelza felt as though her arms and legs were made of overcooked spaghetti. Her voice was as husky as Mr Greensplat's after all the screaming and shouting on the many, many rides they had been on. Her favourite so far was The Rocket, a ride with a rocket shaped carriage on the end of each of its two long arms. They span around like two hands on a clock, always exactly six hours apart. Each time it swung up she felt as though they were rocketing up into space leaving their stomachs behind, when the ride dropped down, it was as though they were plummeting back down through earth's atmosphere.

They had won a sugar dummy, two mood rings, and a wind-up set of chattering teeth on Hook-a-Duck, despite the pickled knight constantly offering useless advice from Nessa's backpack. "How would you know?" Nessa had hissed, "you didn't even have arms for six hundred years. Now shush! People are looking."

"My legs are muuuuuush!" said Demelza as they bought two clouds of pink and blue candy floss on wooden sticks.

"If we go on the ghost train next we can sit down for a while," said Nessa. "And we'll still have enough time and dosh for the Ferris Wheel before your dad gets here."

Demelza eyed the ghost train. The paintings decorating the front were very detailed – gory monsters, ghosts, bloody vampires, mouldy mummies and rotting zombies. Screams, deep roars and cackling laughter drifted out of the dark entrance, which was painted like the mouth of a giant Frankenstein's monster. A small train with a red demon face on the front rattled out of the exit tunnel and squealed to a stop. Its passengers tumbled out of their seats as quickly as they could and ran shrieking and giggling from the ride as the waiting queue surged onto the train.

"Two seats left in the last carriage to Hell!" shouted the ride owner. Captain Honkers perched on top of the Hook-a-Duck stall to wait as the man lifted up the safety bar and waved Nessa and Demelza over to the only bench left. It was right at the back, facing backwards. As he fastened them in, Demelza noticed his hands were tattooed with bones, like an x-ray.

"Excuse me, Mister," said Nessa, "is Jack working tonight?"

"Big Jack, or Young Jack?" he asked as he checked all of the safety bars on the carriage.

"Young Jack," said Demelza, "do you know where we can find him?"

"What you should be asking yourselves," he said as he pulled a lever to start the ride, "is when he'll find you!

Mwahahaaaa, Mwahahahahaa, MWAHAHAHAHAAAAAA!"

He took a deep breath to let out a bigger laugh but burst into a coughing fit as the train rattled through the bloodred streamers and into the darkness.

"He was as useful as a chocolate teapot," muttered Nessa as the darkness closed around them like velvet curtains, muffling the screams and music of the fairground and wrapping them in cold, mouldy smelling gloom.

Demelza inched her bum closer to Nessa and linked her arm as people started screaming behind them. Why had everyone else left the seats at the back empty? She couldn't help yelping as cobwebs brushed their heads and huge fuzzy spiders with glowing red eyes bounced over them and faded into the darkness behind the train. She remembered a story she had been told and whispered to Nessa.

"Connan Lenteglos said that a boy disappeared on a ghost train, then twenty years later, he came out of the tunnel in the exact same seat he had been sitting in. He was the same age, but his hair had turned white." She looked up at Nessa, keeping her fingers crossed that she would say Connan was an idiot.

"Connan Lenteg-loser, is an idiot." said Nessa. "I saw him and his mates, Jory and Trevik, messing about by one of the caravans. They'll be in for it if Jack's dad catches them. Mind you..." she whispered, "Someone at my last school told me that story too. Wouldn't it be rad if this is the same ride?"

"Heh-heh, yeah. Heh-heh, super-rad," Demelza squeaked. She scrooched so close to Nessa she was almost sitting on her knee. There was an ear-splitting scream from the front of the ride as the train bashed through doors into a room filled with swooping, shrieking ghosts with glow in the dark faces.

"**Aaargh!** It touched my hair!" screamed a girl behind them, to shrieks and sniggers from the other passengers. Demelza pulled up the hood of her anorak and tucked her bunches inside. She tied the nylon cords under her chin as she ducked the bouncing, swinging ghosts.

"Argh! Hahahaa!" yelled Nessa as two screeching ghosts started following the train, red eyes spinning in their glowing faces as they flew right up to Nessa and Demelza until they were nose to nose.

"Yaaaaaargh!" yelled Demelza. She pushed herself as far back into her seat as she could. Then, as she was about to wriggle out from under the safety bar and run from the train, a floating, grinning face appeared behind the ghosts.

"Jack?"

"Boo!" Jack pulled off a black balaclava and waved a ghost in each hand. He was dressed all in black so that the ghosts seemed to be floating in the darkness.

"We need to talk to you," said Demelza, a little cross at how Jack was grinning despite everything that had happened the day before.

"OK," said Jack as they rattled through another door, "Meet you outside after the ride. IF you survive, mwahahahahahaaaa!"

"Oh, go mwahahahahahaaaa yourself!" muttered Nessa as the doors swung closed and the train climbed upwards through a tunnel full of swooping bats. Vampires threw open the lids of their coffins to screech at the squealing passengers. Demelza scowled and gripped the safety bar so hard her knuckles turned white. She ignored the rest of the ghosts, ghouls and monsters that swooped, pranced and scurried around them, thinking only about telling Jack he was the world's biggest liar-liar pants on fire.

Nessa bought hotdogs with onions when they got off the ride. She put an extra big squeeze of mustard on hers because she didn't like tomato sauce. They sat on an overturned lemonade crate to eat as they waited for Jack. Demelza tried her best to stay angry as she munched hers and fought off Captain Honkers, who kept trying to peck the wormlike strands of boiled onions from the top.

"Hey!" called Jack with a friendly grin as he popped out of a door in the side of the ghost train. He was back in his jeans and t-shirt. "Why don't we talk on the Ferris…"

BANG!

A loud, echoing explosion rang out as the sky was sprayed with multicoloured sparks. Captain Honkers flapped down into the safety of Demelza's arms with a loud HONK!

Pop-pop-POP, wheeeeeeeeeeeee, BOOM!

"Fireworks!" Demelza gasped. Bright lights whizzed and swirled and exploded in huge colourful starbursts above them. "Where are they coming from?"

A loud boom was followed by the sound of crashing rocks and distant screams.

"The quarry!" Jack yelled. "Come on!"

Chapter Seven
ROCK JAIL

BOOM! *Pop-pop-pop,* *BANG!*

Fireworks danced across the sky above the fairground and nearby quarry. Demelza felt as though she and Nessa were soldiers charging into battle with pretty much everyone who had been at the fair. Captain Honkers flew above their heads, keeping close as explosions lit the sky. People screamed and shouted as they fell over or tried to find their friends and families. She wished they had brought their bikes as they ran through the crowd, trying to keep an eye on Jack. The pickled knight let out little grunts and ye olde rude words as he bounced around inside Nessa's backpack.

"What is happening?" he yelled. **"Has the end of the world come at last?"**

"Quiet!" snapped Nessa as people turned to stare.

They managed to dodge the chain of fair folk forming in front of the rusty fence covered in warning signs at the entrance to the quarry.

"Watch your step," said Nessa as they scrambled over the fence and made their way carefully down the stony slope, tangled with weeds and roots, into the disused quarry. It looked more like a spooky garden in the twilight, trees and ivy clawing their way out of dark crevices. The tor above them was silhouetted against the setting sun. The fireworks had fizzled out, but through the tangle of weeds and bushes they could see flames leaping from a cardboard box half crushed by rocks that had cascaded down the walls. Jack, his dad - Big Jack - and a huddle of fair folk were staring at the rock pile, their faces white.

"Help! Helllllp!" yelled distant voices from behind the rocks.

"Connan!" said Demelza. Of course it was Connan. Who else would spoil everyone else's fun by doing something stupid? She clambered onto the rock pile and stared down through a gap between the larger boulders. Three frightened faces peered up at her.

"Get back," said Big Jack, lifting her down. "Those rocks could fall onto them. We've got to be careful."

"It's Connan, Jory and Trevik," Demelza told Nessa as the fair folk assessed the rockfall.

"They must have set all the fireworks off at once," said Nessa. "No wonder they caused a rockfall."

"Are you hurt?" a tall, black woman with hair wound into long tight braids plaited together down her back called down to the boys with a French accent. Demelza guessed she was Jack's mum as she waved him over to put the fire out.

"Just get us out!" Connan shouted. "The caves behind us are blocked. We're running out of air!"

"No, you're not, lame-brain!" called Nessa. "The hole you're talking through is letting in air!" She rolled her eyes at Demelza and noticed Jack's mum trying not to laugh. The fair folk formed a chain and began carefully removing rocks from the top of the pile. They passed them from one to another to form a pile at the end of the chain. Their faces were pale and they worked with grim determination. Demelza sensed an unspoken fear.

"Your friends will be alright," said Jack's mum, climbing down to join them as Jack stamped out the little flames. "They're not hurt. We'll have them out safely soon."

"They're NOT our friends," said Demelza firmly, horrified at the thought of anyone assuming she could be friends with Connan and his little gang.

"And we really don't mind if you want to leave them in there," said Nessa.

65

"Noted," said Jack's mum, "but I think maybe we should rescue them all the same. I'm Rose. You must be Nessa and Demelza, Jack's new friends?"

"That's us," grinned Demelza, happy to hear that Jack had told his mum they were friends. "And this is Captain Honkers," she added, picking up the goose under one arm..

"If everything is OK, why do they all look so worried?" asked Nessa, nodding towards the fair folk.

"Demelza Penrose!" a loud voice boomed around the quarry.

"Uh-oh," said Demelza. Rose melted away to join the chain removing rocks as Demelza gave a half wave to her dad as he strode down the track towards them. "Hi Dad," she squeaked.

"Don't hi Dad me, as if you hadn't broken into a quarry and gone running towards a rockfall. You two were supposed to wait for me. And where's Mr Calenick? Did you forget about him too?" Nessa gave her backpack a quick nudge as she heard the pickled knight clear his throat to answer.

"Whoa!" shouted Big Jack. They turned to see him braced against a large rock that threatened to roll down onto the boys.

Demelza's dad ran to help him push the boulder safely down and away from the trapped boys. All three were screaming to be pulled out of their rocky prison as little stones trickled down onto them. The chain of rock shifters sped up and soon Big Jack, Rose and Demelza's dad were reaching into the cave and pulling out three dirty, bruised boys who looked very sorry for themselves.

"It wasn't me," shouted Connan, before anyone could say a word, "Jory took the fireworks!"

Jory gave him a shove.

"It was Trev's idea!"

"Shut up!" growled Trevik, "you're the one who set them all off at once!"

"That," said Big Jack, "was the stupidest thing I've ever seen, and I've seen plenty of stupid. I ought to call the police to deal with you."

The quarry suddenly echoed with three voices pleading for mercy, apologising, and promising to behave for ever and ever.

"As if they'd call the police," Nessa whispered to Demelza. "They're lying just like they did last night."

"But we're not going to call the police," said Rose firmly.

"Told you," Nessa nudged Demelza. "They've definitely got something funny going on."

"I reckon they're in enough trouble already," said Demelza's dad as shouting broke out at the entrance to the quarry. A cluster of adults with very red faces broke through the blockaded entrance, pushed aside the fencing and charged down towards them. Demelza was pretty sure she could see steam pouring from their ears.

"CONNAN LENTEGLOS!"
"TREVIK POLGOOTH!"
"JORY HAYLE!"

Demelza grabbed Nessa and dived out of the path of the angry ball of parents rolling towards them. She wondered if she was the only one to notice a shadowy figure detach itself from the group and disappear behind a huge, moss

covered rock. Connan, Jory and Trevik were frozen to the spot. The mob swirled around the boys, checking to make sure they were weren't injured, then one by one they were grabbed by their parents and marched out of the quarry. Promises of confiscated computers, an end to pocket money and lifetime fairground bans drifted back on the evening breeze.

Big Jack and Rose shook hands with Demelza's dad and thanked him for his help. As they talked, Demelza and Nessa dragged Jack to a quiet spot. Out of the corner of her eye Demelza saw a familiar arm beckoning them from behind the mossy rock.

"No games. What's going on?" asked Nessa.

"What do you mean?" said Jack. "Those lads nicked the opening night fireworks and got themselves trapped. We just saved them."

"Then why do your mum and dad look like it's the end of the world?" said Demelza, "And why are they still digging?" she pointed at the fair folk still frantically pulling aside rocks. "There's caves behind there. I know 'cos Dad said he went down there with Mum. Connan said they're blocked now. So, what do you know about the caves?"

"Please, leave it," said Jack.

"No," said Nessa. "You made us look like daft little kids telling fibs to the police last night. Ren jumped off a cliff into the sea. We saw it, and you lied about it."

Jack shook his head.

"Nope! Don't you dare lie again." said Demelza as he opened his mouth to speak. "We KNOW it was Ren. That CAN'T have been her that the police saw when they visited you. Who pretended to be her? Why did she jump? Why are you pretending she's alive?"

"OK, Mum's friend pretended to be her last night," said Jack, "but she's totally fine, honest!"

"I said, NO LIES!" Demelza waggled her finger in his face as Captain Honkers snapped at his ankles.

Honk!

"Ow! Call him off!" Jack danced from foot to foot as Captain Honkers honked and pecked and pecked and honked. "I'm not lying, honest! Look!" He pointed up at the fence. Ren was standing behind it, hand over her mouth as she stared at the blocked caves.

"That impossible," said Nessa. She grabbed Jack's t-shirt. "Tell us what's going on, or we'll find out ourselves and tell everyone."

"Yeah," said Demelza. "We'll find out what's in the caves too." She remembered what her dad had told her the night before. "I know there's a giant cavern down there, and I reckon there's another way in."

"You two!" said Demelza's dad, "back to the car, pronto!" He picked Captain Honkers up under his arm. "We need to have words. Words about trust."

"Yes Dad. Sorry Dad," said Demelza meekly, as Nessa kicked her backpack behind the rock that had been trying to get their attention. Nessa coughed loudly to cover the sound of the bag being unzipped, followed by a rather squelchy noise, a bit like a severed head being clumsily plonked back onto a neck stump.

"Mr Calenick! We're sorry for running away and leaving you at the fairground," said Nessa loudly, as the pickled knight emerged from behind the rock, head fixed firmly on his shoulders with a tightly tied scarf. Jack grabbed Nessa and Demelza as the pickled knight made a big show of apologising to Demelza's dad for losing sight of the girls.

"Look, did you mean that?" whispered Jack. "You know about the cavern? There's another way in?"

"I know loads of Penfurzy secrets," said Demelza. "Dad said there's a legend about it and everything. Mum was looking for the way in, through the quarry, and through somewhere near the harbour. I bet she wrote about it in her notebooks."

Jack bit his lip and glanced over his shoulder to make sure his parents weren't listening. They weren't. They were pulling at the rocks with the others.

"Tomorrow. Ten o' clock. I'll meet you at the arcade."

"Won't you be working at the fair?" asked Nessa.

"The fair will be closed," said Jack. "There are things we need to prepare in case…" he paused. "Look, I'll tell you everything tomorrow. I need your help. Penfurzy, and maybe the world, depends on us!"

Chapter Eight
ALL OF THE JACKS

Jack was already waiting outside the arcade when Demelza and Nessa cycled into town with Captain Honkers perched between Demelza's wide handlebars, snapping at any flies that buzzed by. Demelza's Dad had only let her out to meet Nessa after she promised she'd be home for lunch. Jack wasn't his usual smiling self. There were shadows under his eyes.

"You look like you've been up all night," said Nessa as Neon Justice skidded to a stop next to Rogue Avenger.

"Pretty much," said Jack. "Is there somewhere we can talk?" he looked around the busy street. "Somewhere we won't be overheard?"

Nessa looked at Demelza, "Tortuga?"

Demelza nodded. "Tortuga. Follow us!"

Jack cycled after Demelza and Nessa as they led the way to the harbour and followed a track up to the top of the sand dunes. They left their bikes on the grass and followed a sandy path down between the dunes.

"Through here," Nessa clambered over a dry fence of driftwood and through the tall grasses.

"Behold!" Demelza parted the grass to reveal an overturned fishing boat. Its paint had peeled away and the hull was covered in sun bleached barnacle shells. A hand painted pirate flag flew proudly from a driftwood post next to it. A sign nailed to the post read:

Tortuga

Pirate refuge

Penfurzy Rebel Bicycle Club Members Only!

"It's fine, you can come in without the password," Demelza told Jack as he read the sign. "You're with all four members and we all say you can come in."

"Four?" said Jack as he was half led, half pushed through the sharp-edged grass around to the other side of the boat.

"Yes," said Demelza. "Me, Nessa, Honkers, an'… ow!" Nessa's backpack bounced into Demelza's arm as something inside it shushed her. Nessa lifted a sheet of wood to reveal a hole, reinforced with the sides of a wooden tea crate, that led down under the rim of the boat. Demelza climbed into it and slithered down into a dugout hideaway under the overturned boat, its sandy walls supported with driftwood, rusty signs and salvaged wood. She put on her headtorch to light the cosy wooden cave as Jack and Nessa wriggled down after her.

"Wow. Rad den!" said Jack, looking up at the inside of the boat that gave the appearance of church rafters.

"Welcome to Tortuga," Demelza announced. "It's named after a…"

"Famous pirate island," said Jack. "Good name. Tortuga means turtle, and your boat looks like a turtle sitting in the sand. Mum was born in Haiti," he smiled as Demelza stared at him, open mouthed, "That's where Tortuga is."

"Oh," said Demelza, grudgingly impressed. "Yes, all of that." She was surprised Nessa hadn't chimed in with one of her wild stories about being the captain of a pirate ship before coming to Penfurzy. She hadn't told any of her stories for a while. Demelza didn't really believe them all, but she quite missed them.

"Right, let's get down to business," said Nessa. She tucked her backpack behind the milk crate they used as both a seat and a table as Captain Honkers made himself comfortable on top of it. "Talk, Jack! What's going on with Ren, the fair and the caves in the quarry?"

Jack sighed and leaned back against the hull, biting his lip as if unsure whether to speak.

"Spill!" shouted Demelza.

HONK! agreed Captain Honkers.

"I'm wondering where to start," Jack twisted the end of the bandana he wore as a headband. "OK, there's a reason we come back here, and many other places all over the world, every ten years. We have to. If we don't, something terrible will happen."

Demelza scrooched closer, her head torch lighting him so that he cast a giant shadow onto the boat above them.

"You said your mum heard a legend about a giant cavern deep under the island. Did you mean… big?"

"Yes," said Demelza.

"Huge! Gigantic! Is it real? Do you know what's in it?"

Jack nodded. He pointed up at his shadow.

"Shadows," gasped Demelza, "Man-eating shadows that reach out and grab you?"

"No! Not shadows," Jack leant towards them, face deadly serious as he whispered. "Giants. It really is a giant cavern."

Demelza and Nessa stared at him, then at each other. Demelza broke first and the two of them snorted with laughter.

"Stop it," Jack gave them both a shove. "Stop laughing. I'm serious! There are five of them. Sleeping right here, under Penfurzy."

"Yeah, I get it," said Nessa, "You're Jack, from Jack and the Beanstalk, right?"

"Or Jack the Giant Killer?" giggled Demelza. Jack wasn't laughing.

"That was my great-times-thirty grandad," he said. "Dad is Jack the Giant Slayer now, then it will be me. But we don't kill them. We haven't for centuries. We put them to sleep."

They stopped laughing.

Nessa stared at him, long and hard.

Demelza cocked her head to one side. He didn't look like someone who was telling lies. She thought about it. Jack would probably laugh if they told him they'd found a castle full of medieval ghosts under the sea, or met a long dead king beneath the Piskie Parc Whiplash Whirligig rollercoaster.

"Giants. You're serious?" said Nessa.

"Deadly," said Jack. "My family has travelled the world for hundreds of years, keeping them from waking up and eating and destroying everything. We have to travel in a way that doesn't raise suspicion. That's why we have a fairground."

"And I guess that's how you earn money to keep travelling all over the world?" said Nessa

Jack looked a bit awkward.

"Money's not really a problem. Before we became a fair, we were a travelling theatre. My grandma told me our history. She was a Jack too. If people found out there are bloodthirsty giants sleeping in caves all over the world they'd panic, or worse, make them into weapons."

"What do you mean, you put them to sleep?" asked Demelza. "How?"

"That's where Ren comes in," said Jack. "You've heard her sing right? She can sing a song that makes them sleep for ten years. It doesn't harm them. Women from her family have always travelled with the Jacks – to help us protect the world from giants, and giants from the world."

"What happens if they wake up?" asked Demelza.

"Then have to stop them," said Jack. "Before they start to eat. The more they eat, the bigger and more bloodthirsty they get."

"The tremors," said Nessa, "that's the giants?"

Jack nodded. "We're behind schedule with what happened in Japan. The giants are getting restless. If Ren doesn't sing to them very soon, they'll wake up and wipe out Penfurzy."

"That's why you were all so upset about the caves," said Demelza. "You use them to get down into the caverns?"

"Yep," said Jack. "But now they're blocked. There's no way through. Mum, Dad and the others are preparing for the worst, but I thought you might be able to help us find a way in for Ren."

"We'll help," said Demelza. She checked her watch. "But I promised Dad we'd be back for lunch. Come with us, I'll check Mum's notebooks for maps of the tunnels."

"Thanks," said Jack. "If there's a way, I bet you two can find it."

HONK! said Captain Honkers.

"Sorry, you three!" said Jack.

Nessa's backpack coughed.

"Um, make that four," said Nessa. She undid the zips and reached inside her bag. "Jack, I'd like you to meet…" she pulled out the pickled knight's bearded bonce and placed it on the sand in front of her, "Sir Calenick, Penfurzy Knight. Well, part of him."

Jack pushed himself up against the hull, eyes almost popping out of his sockets as the blue-tinged head rocked forwards to gobble up a small crab scuttling across the den floor. He looked up at Jack, crab legs wriggling in one corner of his mouth. He munched down his crunchy snack, burped and gave a little bow,

"Sorry, force of habit. Delighted to meet you, Jack. I have heard legends of your family. We would be honoured to help you in your quest!"

Chapter Nine
BENEATH PENFURZY

"It's OK. He doesn't bite," said Demelza as they pulled their bikes up by the shed behind her house and Nessa lifted the pickled knight out of her backpack.

"I'll take your word for it," said Jack, leaning away from the severed head as Demelza unlocked the shed door.

"This way, Bod!" called the pickled knight as his headless body blundered out of the shed, hands outstretched.

"I still don't get how it can find and hear you," said Nessa as the body grasped the pickled knight and plonked him onto its shoulders.

"But you're A-OK with him being able to take his head on and off?" said Jack, as Demelza wrapped a scarf tightly around the pickled knight's neck to cover the join between head and body.

"There you go, Mr Calenick," said Demelza, patting him on the shoulder.

"You have my gratitude," said the pickled knight. He grabbed a mop. "Now, I must away. The toilet block calls to me."

"Nothing weird about that," said Jack, watching him hurry off, followed by Captain Honkers. "Yup, toootally normal."

Demelza's dad had made sandwiches and a hot batch of saffron buns for lunch.

"These are SO good, Mr Penrose," said Jack as he cut open a steaming bun and buttered the yellow, curranty insides.

"Thank you, Jack," said Demelza's dad. "I checked in with Mrs Lenteglos this morning. The boys are fine. They've been grounded and won't be back at the fairground for the rest of the time you're here."

"Dad will be pleased," said Jack, "He's got enough to worry about."

"Everything OK? There a sign in town saying the fairground isn't open today."

"Dad has… stuff to prepare," said Jack uneasily.

"We're finished now, Dad," said Demelza, giving their plates a super quick rinse under the tap. "We'll be in my caravan if you need us!"

"What's your dad preparing?" Nessa asked Jack as Demelza herded them through the field of marauding snot goblins and into her little caravan.

"There's a reason we're a travelling fair," said Jack, as Demelza slithered under her bed to pull out a box full of her mother's notebooks. "The rides aren't just rides. They're traps. Traps and weapons."

Demelza dropped the box.

"Weapons?" repeated Nessa.

"For catching giants," said Jack. "I've only seen them used once, in Mauritius after we were delayed in Japan. A small giant woke up, but we caught it with… you know that ride, The Rocket?"

"The one with two rockets that **WHOOOOSH** up then shoot down?" said Demelza. "It made my legs feel like liquorice laces!"

"That's the one. A couple of adjustments and it turns into a catapult that can throw things for miles. We used it to drop a huge weighted net over the giant while he was staggering around, dazzled by the sun after smashing his way out of the cave. Then the Meteorite ride… you saw the black and white swirl pattern on the bottom? That tips over into a big spinning hypno-wheel. It has lights and sounds to send giants into a trance. We hypnotised him then led him back down to the cave with the others. Ren sang them back to sleep and we had to spend days blocking up the smashed entrance. There are A LOT of giants in the world, but the ones in Penfurzy are the biggest and meanest. The net won't slow these ones down. If they wake up and get out, well, let's just make sure it doesn't happen."

"How do you know they're mean?" asked Demelza as she opened the box of notebooks.

"Yeah," added Nessa. "Isn't it cruel to keep them sleeping for hundreds of years?"

Jack sighed. "I know it sounds bad, but if they got free they'd destroy everything, eat every living thing they find. The army would turn up with tanks and rocket launchers. Then they'll hunt down the rest until every single one is gone forever. If we keep them sleeping, then when humans go extinct, or move to another planet, the giants will wake up and have the place to themselves."

"He's right," said Nessa. "I read in a magazine that the government has secret places full of aliens that got locked up after they crash-landed on earth. If they don't kill all the giants, I bet they'd take your Meteorite machine and hypnotise them to fight in our wars. We'll help you, for the sake of the giants, as well as us. D, what have you got?

Demelza rummaged through her mother's mystery and adventure notebooks.

"Spriggans, Piskies, Pendragons…" Demelza pulled out book after book, "The Treasure of the Penfurzy Knights…"

"Remind us to tell you about that one," said Nessa to Jack, "Y'know, if we're not all gobbled up by giants tomorrow."

"Ooh, here!" Demelza grabbed a green notebook labelled Below Penfurzy – Caves, Caverns and Secret Spaces.

"Whoa," Nessa flipped through pages and pages of carefully drawn maps of Penfurzy with tracing paper over the top to show the caves that ran below it. "Look, there's a tunnel from the windmill's cellar right down to the harbour!"

"Wow," Demelza traced the tunnel from Nessa's house on her mother's carefully drawn map. "I bet it's an old smuggler's tunnel. We should explore it and see if they left anything interesting behind."

Jack coughed loudly. "Could we look for the way to the giants first?"

"Oh yeah." An envelope fell out of the notebook. Demelza picked up and absent-mindedly stuffed it into the front pocket of her dungarees then flicked through the notebook to the maps of the north of the island. There were a few pages where her mum had sketched images of where she thought the cavern might be, and how big it was.

"She nearly has it here," said Jack, pointing to a spot between the quarry and the park. "Only the cavern is at least twice the size she thought it was."

"Twice the size?" said Demelza "That's humongous!"

"The fairground is right above it," said Nessa.

"That's so we can listen," said Jack. "You saw the horn next to Ren's caravan? It's really sensitive listening equipment. That's why Dad got so annoyed when you went near it."

"Ohhhh," said Demelza. "So it's not an earthquake machine!"

"Nope. It's an early warning system," said Jack. "But now we don't need it to know they're going to wake up very, very soon."

As if planned, the earth shivered. They all flopped to the floor, heads together as they searched the notebook for any sign of a tunnel that led to the cavern.

Jack traced the tunnel from the quarry with his finger, "Looks as though your mum managed to get through some of the things we put in to trick people into turning back, like the false wall, right here. She found her way down to the underground lake. I didn't think anyone had ever been that far down, except us." He smiled at Demelza. "I'm impressed!"

Demelza nodded. "She was very clever." She was amazed at how many caves and tunnels her mum had mapped out under the island. Beneath Penfurzy was a rabbit warren of caves and tunnels. Natural caves, mine shafts, tunnels for smugglers, sea caves, ancient burial mounds.

"It's no good," said Jack at last. He sat up and rubbed the carpet marks on his elbows. "Some of these tunnels pass close by, but she didn't find a way in. This one from the caves near the harbour looks good, but it comes to a dead end." He closed his eyes and rubbed his forehead with his fingertips. "There's nothing for it. We need to get everyone off the island, including you. Me, Dad, Mum and the rest of the crew, we need to fight."

"No," said Nessa, "There's got to be a way where no one, even giants, get hurt, and the Penfurzy Rebel Bicycle Club is going to help you find it. D and I know someone who knows more about living under Penfurzy than any human." She raised an eyebrow and looked at Demelza. "Do you think he'll help us? If we can find him?"

There was only one person Nessa could mean.

"One way to find out," Demelza grabbed her rucksack and packed torches, string, chalk, some snacks and the notebook. "Let's go spriggan hunting!"

Chapter Ten
ADVENTURE AND VALIANT COMPANIONS

Demelza's headtorch lit the wall of the cavern deep below Piskie Parc's Whiplash Whirligig as a scrabbling noise came from within.

"Better get back," said Nessa, pulling Jack out of the way as roots slithered out of the wall like gigantic brown worms. They flopped into a pile on the floor then rose up, writhing as they took on a human shape. Arms, legs, a huge head with a wide, thin lipped slit of a mouth. Jack's own mouth was open as if screaming, but only a tiny squeak of air escaped.

The creature opened its mouth and roared, deep and loud. The sound vibrated through Demelza to the ends of her frizzy hair.

As the roar faded and the cave was silent again, the creature turned to them, sharp brown teeth glinting in the torchlight as its mouth twisted into a half grin, half grimace.

"Hello, Mr Spriggan," Demelza gave the creature a little curtsey.

"Looking sharp," said Nessa with a tiny nod. Jack seemed to be trying to merge into the wall behind him.

"This is Jack," said Demelza, pushing him forwards. "Say hello to nice Mr Spriggan, Jack."

"Huh, Huh-hi?" croaked Jack.

"And you remember Pickles?" Nessa pulled the pickled knight out of her rucksack by the hair.

"SIR Calenick!" said the pickled knight, dropping to the floor and headbutting her shin.

"It is barely six moon cycles since you invaded my last home," hissed the spriggan in a voice like rustling leaves. "Yet here you are again, disturbing those who dwell in the dark when greater terrors stir deep below this land."

"We know," said Nessa, "that's why we came to find you. We need your help to stop them. Tell him, Jack."

Jack pulled himself together enough to nod. "The giants, we can stop them, but the tunnel from the quarry has collapsed. We need another way to get to them before they wake up."

Demelza handed the spriggan a map page she had very carefully removed from her Mum's notebook.

"We're sure there's a way through this cave system.'

"And why should I help him?" The spriggan asked. It stared at Jack, amber eyes screwed up into suspicious slits.

"I know your bloodline. I can smell it. It is a violent one, stemming from blood and greed."

"I know," said Jack. "The first Jacks only cared about getting rich and being famous and feared. That was a long, long time ago. Now my family protects people from the giants, and protects the giants from people. But if we don't get to them soon they'll wake up. And if we can't stop them, that will be the end of humans."

"And that's bad because…?" asked the spriggan. "Noisy, destructive beasts. Why shouldn't they be wiped out by creatures even more destructive? Creatures who have been around far longer than them?"

Nessa stepped forward and cleared her throat. "Once they've eaten all the people and animals on Penfurzy, what comes next?" she asked. "It shouldn't take much for them to rip the top off your home here, like cracking open an Easter egg to eat the treats inside. And if you think humans are noisy, imagine big stomping footsteps shaking the whole island while they fight each other."

Earth trickled down the walls as the ground beneath them gave a shiver at the perfect moment.

"And they'd throw giant boulders around, just for fun," added Jack. "Then the army, navy and airforce will come here and probably destroy the island while trying to destroy them."

The spriggan stroked its chin with a sound like scraping tree bark, as it stood deep in thought.

"I suppose you did return the Penfurzy cup to the Great King's tomb," it said.

"And we rebuilt your cairn for you," said Demelza, "after we pulled it apar…"

"Yep!" said Nessa quickly. "We rebuilt it after some accident, completely unrelated to us, happened to it. So, you'll help us? You'll tell us how to get to the giants" cavern?"

"I'll help you," said the spriggan, "IF, you promise never to take advantage of my good nature again.

"Done," said Demelza. She spat on her hand and held it out to the spriggan.

"Bodily fluids are not required to seal this agreement," said the spriggan, recoiling from Demelza's dripping hand, "Urgh, humans!" He peered at the page Demelza had given him. "I do not know of a way, but my cousins might. I will speak to them."

His hands and arms turned to wriggling roots and squirmed back into the crack he had emerged from.

The rain was coming down fast as Demelza and Nessa said goodbye to Jack and cycled at full speed from Piskie Parc back to the caravan park. Thunder rumbled in the distance. Demelza should have guessed a storm was coming when Captain Honkers refused to leave the shower block and join their quest.

Demelza's dad was getting into the car to go out searching for them when they cycled into the caravan park, tired, muddy and dripping wet. The caravan park was quiet, all of the caravan doors closed, the netted windows of each lit with a cosy yellow glow as the tourists sheltered from the rain.

"Sorry we're late, Dad," said Demelza, leaning her bike against the shed and giving him a soggy hug. "We thought we'd be safer sheltering from the storm than riding through it."

Nessa nodded.

"Sorry Mr Penrose. We'd have called, but there was no phone-box nearby."

Demelza's dad looked at them as though trying to work out whether they were being cheeky or not.

"Demelza knows I don't like her out in this sort of weather, but the storm was sudden so I suppose you did the right thing," he said as he herded them into the kitchen, where a fire was roaring away in the hearth. "Those tremors don't make cycling in the wet very safe. The news reckons it's something to do with deep sea mining, but I'm not so sure. Honkers has been hiding behind the shower curtains since the last one. Maybe you two can convince him to come out when you get cleaned up."

Nessa sneaked off to the shed to return the pickled knight's head to his body while Demelza checked on Captain Honkers. He was so happy to see her that he wouldn't leave her knee even when she went to the toilet. Her dad had called Nessa's parents to tell them she was staying over rather than anyone having to head out in the wet weather, but, much to Demelza's annoyance, he insisted that they sleep in the main house, rather than her caravan where they could play noisy videogames and have a midnight feast. In the end, they were too tired anyway and had to prod each other awake as they read Demelza's new Whizzo and Flips comic and filled in a mail order form for x-ray specs and invisible ink pens, wondering if Penfurzy would still exist by the time they arrived in the post.

"Shouldn't we be doing something to get ready for tomorrow?" Demelza asked as they got into opposite ends of her bed.

"There's nothing we can do," yawned Nessa as Captain Honkers pattered around to make a nest between them on top of the duvet. "Except rest and hope the spriggan comes back to us. You heard Jack, his family have been preparing for the giants to wake up for hundreds of years. I'm sure they're ready for this."

Demelza lay awake for a while, listening to Nessa's snores as she stared at the stars her nightlight cast on to the ceiling. She wondered if this was the last time she'd ever lie snug and safe in bed, knowing that she'd see the sun rise tomorrow. Maybe there was something she had missed in her mum's notebook? She leaned out of bed, moving gently so as not to disturb Nessa as she reached for her crumpled dungarees on the floor. Captain Honkers wriggled as the cover shifted under him. He tucked his head further under his wing and snuggled back down as Demelza pulled the notebook out of her front pocket, an envelope fluttered to the floor. She picked it up and recognised her mum's gently sloping handwriting on the front.

To Demelza

She pulled a spare blanket over her head to make a tent and switched on her torch. She quietly opened the envelope and pulled out a letter on space themed writing paper. It had a little drawing of Demelza and her mum and dad floating around in spacesuits in the top corner. She began to read...

My darling Demelza,
I am writing this while you are asleep on the
sofa next to me, cuddling an abandoned gosling
you saved from the reeds this morning

Demelza smiled. That was the day she met Captain Honkers.
He had decided she was his new mum and pretty much lived in
her pocket for the next few weeks.

I am so proud to be your mother and to witness
your growing sense of adventure. I have put all
of my notes on Penfurzy's mysteries into these
notebooks and know you will enjoy learning
about them just as much as I do. I can't wait
for us to explore them together.

Demelza's heart gave a little lurch. Her eyes prickled with
tears as she wished her mum was there to give her a big hug
and say that everything would be OK. Her mum would know
what to do, where to look for the way down below Penfurzy.

I wish you as much happiness in your life as
you bring me every day. I know you will have

a life filled with adventure and valiant companions. You are clever and strong, I know you will face any challenge with confidence, and have the wisdom to choose your battles and to take risks with care.

Listen to your heart and don't ever be afraid to share your thoughts and feelings. Your dad and I love you so very much. Even if we live on different sides of the world one day, I will always be with you, in your freckles, the colour of your eyes, your wild red hair, and in your heart.

With all of my love, now and forever,

Mum xxx

Demelza held in a sob as she wiped her eyes and nose on her pyjama sleeve. Why didn't you take risks with care, Mum? She thought to herself as she turned off her torch and lay down with a sigh. Then you'd still be here, helping us work out what to do next. She hugged the letter close to her heart until she finally drifted off to sleep.

The sun was still hitting snooze on its alarm clock when a scratching noise worked its way into Demelza's dreams.

"Psst, wake up!" Nessa shook her shoulder gently. "It's back."

Demelza sat up and gently touched her finger to Captain Honker's beak to stop him from honking. She shuffled down the mattress to look out of the window with Nessa. The branches of the tree outside were scratching and squeaking down the glass. No, not branches – a hand with long, gnarled fingers beckoning them. Demelza's eyes followed the arm to a figure sitting in the tree. The spriggan. She opened the window and it shrank down to the size of small monkey and leapt onto the ivy growing up the wall of the house and clambered up to the windowsill.

"Keep your feathered beast away from me," it snarled as Captain Honkers stuck his head out to hiss in its face.

"Go back to sleep, Honkers," said Demelza, plonking him back in his duvet nest.

"Did you find the way?" asked Nessa.

The spriggan nodded and handed back the page Demelza had given it.

"I have spoken to every spriggan and piskie on this island. Your mother was right about the caves. To get to the cavern you will need a boat, and an iron will."

"Then it's a good job we have both," said Demelza with a smile.

Chapter Eleven
FLUUURP, BLOP-BLOP-BLOP

"Why did you tell Dad you can drive?" Demelza shouted from the back seat of her dad's car, over the sound of grinding gears.

"Because," said the pickled knight as his body wrestled with the steering wheel, "I was the best horseman in the Penfurzy Knights." He kept one hand firmly on the wheel and crunched through the gears as the car lurched along the country road to the fairground. "And if I can tame a wild stallion and ride it into battle, then I can tame this metal beast!"

"Those two things are not the same at all," sighed Nessa, plonking her boombox into the footwell to protect it from Captain Honkers who kept pecking at the buttons. "You can't learn to drive by taming a car! You need lessons and…"

"You must make haste to share your information with the Jacks," the pickled knight shouted over her. "Mr Penrose is busy, so I have chosen to escort you fair maidens… ahem, bold warriors," he quickly corrected himself, "on your mission. Perhaps you would prefer to travel by foot?"

"Fine!" Nessa shouted over electric guitars. "Just keep your hands on the wheel and your head on your neck!"

Demelza was glad the roads weren't too busy at the north of the island now that the fair had closed. The pickled knight still hadn't grasped the concept of sticking to the correct side of the road.

"Look OUT!" she grabbed Mr Calenick's head by the ears and wrenched it around so that he could see the armoured van swerving towards them.

"Egads!" screamed the pickled knight, slamming on the brakes and wrestling with the wheel as the car slid off the road and through the tall grass, mud spraying up the sides. Demelza let out a breath as they skidded to a stop, the front bumper barely an inch from a huge oak tree. The pickled knight's head flew from his shoulders, bounced off the windscreen and jumped angrily back onto his body.

"That's Jack, and his dad!" said Nessa as a truck cabin roared past them in hot pursuit of the van. "Something's happening. Follow them!"

"As the oldest and wisest among us," began the pickled knight, "I don't think we should be…"

"FOLLOW THEM!" yelled Demelza and Nessa, shaking his seat.

HONK-HONNNNK! insisted Captain Honkers.

"Quick-quick-quick-quick-quick!" Demelza shouted over the roaring engine as the pickled knight coaxed the car up out of the ditch. The armoured van had reached the top of the hill. Jack and his dad were right behind it, their truck almost touching the vans rear bumper as they disappeared from sight.

Tyres screeched as the pickled knight floored the accelerator and joined the chase.

"What are they doing?" said Demelza as they crested the hill to see the truck had pulled alongside the heavy van, nudging against it as they thundered along the narrow road.

"They're trying to push it off the road," gasped Nessa as the Jacks gave the van another nudge.

"The marshes!" said Demelza. "They don't know about the marshes. If they push the van off the road it'll sink! We've got to warn them!"

"Beep the horn!" shouted Nessa.

"What?" said the pickled knight.

"The horn, use it!" yelled Demelza.

"What horn?" the pickled knight's head wobbled with confusion as they bounced towards the duelling vehicles.

"Never mind!" Nessa reached over the back of the seat into the boot, grabbed Demelza's dad's shinty stick and jabbed the centre of the steering wheel with it.

"Arthur's beard!" screamed the pickled knight as the horn blared, but it was too late. The truck nudged the van one more time and it span out of control, skidding off the road to crash through the undergrowth, over the abandoned train track and **_SCHLUUUURP!_** into the marsh. The pickled knight pulled up behind the Jacks' truck on the roadside and they all jumped out.

"What's going on?" Demelza called after the Jacks as they raced towards the van, fists clenched, faces red with anger.

"It's them," shouted Jack, "the same guys who tried to take her in Japan!"

"Stay back!" Nessa shouted as they crossed the tracks and ran towards the van. "It's a marsh, you'll sink!"

"Ren's trapped in the back!" yelled Jack, jumping back onto solid ground. "We've got to get her out before it…"

FLUUURP, BLOP-BLOP-BLOP

The rear end of the heavy van raised up from the ground as the front began to sink into the marsh. The driver and passenger doors flew open and two men leapt out, straight into the marsh.

"Help!" they screamed, as they wriggled and squirmed through the mud. A pale, terrified face appeared at the small tinted window at the back of the van.

"Keys!" Jack's dad shouted at the men. Jack grabbed a stone, leapt up onto the rear bumper of the van and hammered at the lock.

"We'll get you out, Ren!" he yelled.

"KEYS!" Jack's dad roared again to the flopping, flailing men wriggling towards them.

"They're gone. I dropped them!" shouted the driver. "Help us, please!"

"No-no-no!" cried Jack. "There's got to be a way to get her out.

"We can't get the door open," said Nessa as the van dipped further into the marsh. "But we can tow the van out."

"Brilliant," said Jack's dad, "Do you have a rope?"

Demelza rummaged in the boot of her Dad's car for his tow ropes as Jack grabbed one from the truck. The pickled knight and Jack's dad reversed the car and truck slowly down, through the shrubs towards the marsh.

"Stop!" yelled Demelza as the rear tyres touched the train tracks. "You'll get stuck on the line if you go any further!"

Demelza and Nessa fixed one end of their rope tightly to their car, Jack did the same to the truck. The two men were still screaming for help but had grabbed onto shrubs and weren't in immediate danger of sinking. But the van was slipping further into the marsh with every second that passed.

Demelza shoved the other end of the tow rope into Nessa's hands. "You're better at jumping an' stuff, so you do it. But be careful, OK?"

"Always, D," said Nessa. "Ready?" she asked Jack. He gave a grim nod. They looped the tow ropes over their shoulders and each took a running leap at the back of the sinking van. Demelza squeaked as their fingers grasped the bumper, but they managed to pull themselves up onto it. They tied their ropes firmly to the van. Ren watched them nervously through the glass as they made the leap back to solid ground.

"Go!" Demelza slapped the rear window of her dad's car. The pickled knight pushed the pedal to the floor. The truck engine roared as Big Jack did the same. The ropes went tight as the two vehicles strained.

"Come on, come on!" pleaded Jack. The van had stopped sinking but the marsh didn't want to let go of its prize.

Honk. Honnnnnk! honked Captain Honkers, flying over to perch on the van as if his weight would help.

Finally, with a noise like the world's biggest whoopie cushion, the back end of the van splatted down into the marsh. It sent a wave of water, pondweed and mud flowing over the failed kidnappers as it was pulled, inch by inch, from the marsh until it sat on solid ground.

Nessa leapt into the driver's seat and put on the handbrake as Jack jumped onto the rear bumper and wiped the mud from the little window. Ren smiled and said something, but the thick glass blocked out the sound of her voice.

Mr Calenick and Big Jack pulled the men from the mud and trussed them up with the tow ropes until they looked like muddy caterpillars squirming around on the ground.

Jack jumped down and hugged Nessa and Demelza.

"Thank you," he said, hand over his heart. "I don't know what would have happened if you hadn't been here."

"We were coming to tell you something," said Demelza. She pulled out the directions the spriggan had given her. "We've found it! The way into the cavern. But we need to go now."

"You told them?" said his dad sharply, as he worked on the doors with a crowbar.

"We can trust them, Dad." said Jack. "Look, they've found the way, and Ren is safe. We can go into the tunnels, she can sing the giants to sleep. Everything is going to be OK."

"No, Jack. It isn't," his dad dropped the crowbar and ran his hand through his hair. "Without the keys, I can't get Ren out. We need the heavy tools back at camp to cut the door open. It'll take hours and we're out of time. This is it. The giants are waking up and I don't know if anything we have is enough to stop them."

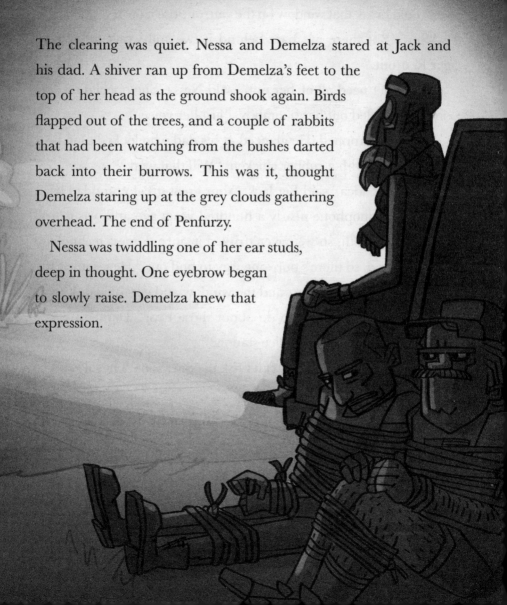

Chapter Twelve
LAYING DOWN TRACKS

The clearing was quiet. Nessa and Demelza stared at Jack and his dad. A shiver ran up from Demelza's feet to the top of her head as the ground shook again. Birds flapped out of the trees, and a couple of rabbits that had been watching from the bushes darted back into their burrows. This was it, thought Demelza staring up at the grey clouds gathering overhead. The end of Penfurzy.

Nessa was twiddling one of her ear studs, deep in thought. One eyebrow began to slowly raise. Demelza knew that expression.

"You have a plan?"

"I have a plan," said Nessa. She looked at Big Jack. "Do you think you could break that window on the van, or prise it out?"

"Sure. But there are bars behind it, we still won't be able to get Ren out."

"We don't need all of her out," said Nessa. She opened the car door and pulled out her boombox. "Just her voice."

Jack's jaw dropped. He glanced at his dad who looked as if he'd been slapped with a rubber chicken. "Will that work?"

"I have no idea,' said Big Jack. 'Your great-great granddad tried it with a gramophone nearly a hundred years ago and was nearly stomped to death, so we haven't risked it since. I guess technology has improved, so there's only one way to find out." He jammed the crowbar into the metal around the window and got to work.

"What are you going to do about those two?" Demelza asked Jack. "Take them to the police station?"

Jack shook his head. "We can't risk the questions. They'll want to know why they tried to kidnap her."

"Why do they keep coming after her?" asked Nessa. One of the men laughed.

"You don't know?" he asked in a thick American accent.

"Shut up!" growled Big Jack, his muscles bulged as he twisted the crowbar. The thick glass pane began to ease out of its frame.

"In there, is a gen-u-ine mermaid. She's wasted on these two-bit carnies. She'll have a better life in our circus than they could ever give her. She'll be rich, and famous! Who doesn't want that?"

"Ren! Ren doesn't want that," shouted Jack.

"A mermaid?" snorted Nessa. "Right dude. You're nuttier than peanut butter."

Jack wasn't laughing.

"It's true. That's why we had to lie to the police. You've seen what happens when people find out. They either want to experiment on her or turn her into a freak show attraction.

"Freak show?" shouted the man. "We ain't no freak show. We're the finest cabinet of curiosities in the yew ess of A. and you, sir, are holding your mermaid back from earning herself, and us, a LOT of money. Sell her to us and you'll be set for life."

"We don't need your money," shouted Jack, pulling off one of his long sports socks. "Ren, doesn't belong to anyone but herself." He stormed over and tied the sock tightly around the man's mouth. "She is not. For. SALE!" He shoved the man back into the dirt. Captain Honkers pattered over to give him a sharp nip on his nose.

"How can she be a mermaid?" asked Nessa. "She's got legs."

"Not when she's in the water," said Jack. "Mermaids can come onto land, but they should spend as much time in seawater as they can. There's a tank full of it in Ren's caravan. And she always goes back to the sea when we're near the coast. Her family live near Penfurzy. She was going to visit them when you saw her. I'm sorry you saw her jump. It must have been frightening."

"Well," said Nessa, as the window popped out of the van with a CRACK and thunked into the earth by Big Jack's feet, "if this works, maybe she can finally go back to the sea." She picked up her boombox. "Let's find out."

She checked the two tapes in the cassette slots and groaned.

"Aw, man. Beatz from the Streetz and Hip-Hop 'Til U Drop, my best mixtapes. Which one gets sacrificed?"

"Neither!" Demelza reached into the glove compartment of her Dad's car and rummaged through the tapes. "Use this. Dad has them all on record anyway."

"Dark Side of The Wall," read Nessa, "Not bad for dad music, but a worthy sacrifice." She shoved it into a cassette slot, then pulled a microphone out of her backpack. She plugged it into the boombox, climbed up onto the bumper and held it through the bars to Ren. "If you sing into here," she mimed singing, "we'll record you on our magic machine."

Ren smiled.

"I'm a mermaid, not an idiot."

"But you've never tried recording your song before?"

Ren shook her head. "You know what will happen if it doesn't work?"

"We know," said Demelza, "but any chance of saving Penfurzy, is worth the risk."

"Wait!" shouted Big Jack as Nessa reached for the record button. He took the microphone from her.

"It works on humans, as well as giants, remember, Jack?" Demelza noticed Jack and his dad exchange a strange look.

"I'll do it. You should get in the car and cover your ears until my signal."

Jack grabbed a pair of ear defenders from the truck and handed them to his dad. That look passed between them again. "Are you sure you'll be OK this close up, Dad?"

"I'll be fine," he put on the ear defenders and gave a thumbs up. "Off you go," he shouted.

Jack wrapped scarves around the heads of the would be kidnappers and followed the others to the car. They closed the doors and rolled up the windows. Nessa shoved Hip-Hop 'Til U Drop into the stereo and pressed play. Her voice filled the car...

Yo-yo-YO! This is DJ Ness on the wheels of steel, bringing you the freshest beats and the raddest...

Nessa leapt for the fast-forward button so fast she knocked the pickled knight's head off.

"Watch it!" he grumbled, leaping back onto his shoulders before Big Jack saw him. Nessa's face glowed so red it seemed to light up the car as she skimmed past her intro and into the music.

"Sweet beats, DJ Ness!" grinned Jack as the music filled the car.

"Look, Ren's started singing," said Nessa quickly.

Demelza watched Ren's lips moving and wondered what her lullaby sounded like. She remembered the beauty of the song she had overheard the day they met Jack and wished they could listen.

"What are you going to do about them?" asked Nessa, pointing at the kidnappers. "Will they leave you alone if you let them go?"

Jack shook his head, his lips set in a thin line.

"They'll keep coming. People like that wouldn't even care if they knew their actions would destroy the world. Not if it makes them money. They won't ever stop."

Ren had finished singing. Big Jack removed his ear defenders and gave them a thumbs up. They jumped out to join him.

"This has never been tried before," he said as the tape rewound. "We don't know what's going to happen. Demelza, Nessa, I need you to tell me how to get to the cavern, and I need to borrow this." He held up the boombox. "Jack, you go get some of the folks from camp to tow the van back. Help them set up the equipment in case this doesn't work. You've done it with me plenty of times, you know what to do."

"Whoa! Hands off the Helix," said Nessa, automatically reaching for the boombox.

"Dad, no disrespect," said Jack, in a tone that Demelza recognised as always leading to something very cheeky, "but that is the stupidest idea I've ever heard. If they wake up, you need to be there at camp. You and Mum made the new equipment, only you two know exactly how it all works. If the giants wake up and you're not both there to stop them, no one will be able to. Let me go to the cavern. Me, Demelza, Nessa and Mr Calenick."

Honk-Honk!

"…and Captain Honkers."

"Jack," said his dad. "I know how hard you've trained. I trust you, but you've just met these girls. You really think they're not going to run screaming from the sight of five giants the height of four double-decker buses?" He looked at Nessa and Demelza. "No offence meant."

Demelza's fingers and toes curled into claws. Nessa looked about to shoot steam from her ears.

"Well, offence taken!" she growled. "Yeah, maybe we've never seen a giant, but have you ever fought an ancient curse?"

"I can't say I hav…"

"Or rode your bike off a cliff onto the tower of a sunken castle?" said Demelza, hands on her hips as she glared up at him.

"Um, no…"

"Or fought ghost armour and dead knights?" said Nessa, arms folded.

"Or had a real live ghost train drive through you on the way to a spooky island in a lake to get a magic cup to save the life of your goose?" asked Demelza, foot tapping.

"I can definitely say no to that one," said Big Jack. He held up his hands as the girls advanced on him.

"Or faced being eaten by an angry spriggan on your way into an ancient tomb to return stolen treasure?" asked Nessa.

"The same spriggan that we visited yesterday, just to get this?" Demelza waved her notebook page and directions she had scribbled down from the spriggan in his face. "To help you!"

"I yield!" said Big Jack. "But did any of that actually happen?"

"Don't take our word for it," said Nessa. Her eyes twinkled as she grabbed the pickled knight by the ears. "He'll back us up." With that she yanked his head off his body and hurled it at Big Jack's chest. He caught it automatically then dropped it with a scream as the pickled knight scowled at him and shouted:

"Never doubt the word of the Penfurzy Rebel Bicycle Club. For they, sir, are the bravest and truest knights this land has ever seen!"

Chapter Thirteen
WAVES AND CAVES

"I've never seen Dad back down so quickly on anything," said Jack as he sat squeezed between Nessa and Demelza in the back of the car as the pickled knight sped them to the harbour, honking the horn furiously as he swerved around the campervans and caravans trundling along the country roads.

"Run screaming," spat Demelza, "us? He's lucky he backed down, or I'd have got Honkers to eat his eyeballs!"

Nessa leaned into Jack and muttered out of the side of her mouth, just as Demelza shouted the same thing:

"Eyeballs is his favourite!"

Honk! Captain Honkers agreed. Eyeballs most certainly were his favourite, but he had so few opportunities to pop them in his beak and guzzle their tasty jelly.

Jack took the map and directions from Demelza. His eyebrows knotted as he tried to understand her writing.

"I know," she sighed. "Dad says my writing looks like a bunch of spiders got drunk, fell in some ink and had a party on a piece of paper."

"He was being kind." Jack turned the paper to see if it made more sense from a different angle.

"Give them here," Nessa scanned the instructions. "It makes perfect sense. We get a boat, sail into this cave in the cliffs, down this narrow tunnel and out into this little cavern. We climb up here, call the piskies, and they'll guide us to the big cavern where the giants are sleeping."

"Piskies?" said Jack, "What are…" he threw up his hands. "It doesn't even matter. Where are we going to get a boat?"

"Right here," said Demelza, as the pickled knight pulled into the carpark by the sand dunes.

"Bod will take the car back," said the pickled knight, leaping off his shoulders and into Nessa's backpack. "I shall come with you."

"How is it driving without a head?" whispered Jack as the pickled knight's body hit the accelerator and roared out of the car park.

"Still trying to work that out," said Nessa.

The wind was picking up and they had to shield their eyes from flying sand as they made their way down through the dunes.

"Tadaaaaa!" said Demelza as they pushed through the grasses to Tortuga.

"Seriously?" said Jack. "You want us to sail this? In this weather? Is it even watertight?"

"We're not going to sail, silly," said Demelza. She handed him two oars. "We'll be rowing."

"Ready?" asked Nessa. Demelza and Jack followed her lead and scrabbled in the sand until they had hold of the rim of the boat.

"Three, two, one... heeeeeeeeave!" They lifted the boat and flipped her over so that she was sitting upright, leaving their den open to the drizzle. Demelza stowed their stack of board games and comics under the crate they used as a seat until they returned with the boat. The earth trembled, sending sand trickling into the den. Demelza swallowed hard. IF they returned.

Captain Honkers flapped into the boat and they all began to push it over the top of the dune and onto a narrow sandy path down through the grass.

"All aboard!" shouted Nessa. She leapt into the boat with her boombox as it began to pick up speed.

"Aye-aye, Captain Ness!" Demelza jumped in behind her and Jack scrambled over the back as the boat sped downhill. They all ducked low to avoid the dry grasses whipping at them as they whizzed through the dunes. Demelza began to sing.

"Row, row, row your boat, quickly down the dunes,"

"If you see a sleeping giant…" Nessa paused and turned to Jack.

"Er, chase it with some spoons?"

"Not bad," said Nessa, "But I'd have gone for, play some sleepy tunes."

"Land ahoy!" shouted Demelza as the boat burst from the grasses and skidded along the sandy beach, scattering tourists in its wake.

"Look out!" Nessa shouted to two snot goblins from the caravan park. The boat smashed through the huge sandcastle they had been building and slid to a stop halfway down the beach.

"So-reee!" Demelza shouted to the goblins as they threw back their heads and wailed.

They all leapt out. Nessa and Jack put their weight behind the boat as Demelza grabbed the frayed rope that hung from the bow and pulled Tortuga all the way down to the sea. Captain Honkers honked encouragement from the boat. Demelza was glad that the tide was on its way in, or they would have had to drag it twice as far.

The skies were still grey as they boarded the boat, but at least the waves were fairly gentle. Nessa and Jack took an oar each as Demelza scanned her little map, Captain Honkers peering over her shoulder.

"It's not too far," said Demelza, "the entrance is the fourth cave round the side of that cliff."

They began to row, Nessa and Jack each trying to out-row the other. Demelza was glad that they both seemed to be as strong as each other, otherwise Tortuga would be travelling in circles instead of heading towards the cliffs.

Demelza unzipped Nessa's backpack so that the pickled knight could jump out. He hopped up onto the bow of the boat and shook out his white hair in the sea breeze. Demelza thought he looked rather like a ship's figurehead, if ships were decorated with big nosed knights rather than beautiful mermaids.

"Perhaps… phew…" Nessa panted, "you could have brought your body to help us row?"

"My body had to return the metal steed I was entrusted with and has cleaning work to catch up with," said the pickled knight, "This way, I am aiding you in your quest as well as carrying out my sworn duties."

"OK," said Demelza, a little uneasily, "as long as Dad doesn't see you without your head."

"Fear not," said the pickled knight, in a voice that made Demelza think that she should definitely be fearing something, "I will stay out of sight, but I have crafted a solution to fool any who glimpse me."

"Which is…?" asked Demelza, dreading the answer.

"A face drawn most skilfully onto a balloon and worn inside a balaclava stitched to my shoulders."

"Of course it is," said Nessa. She shook her head as Demelza hoped that her dad wouldn't ever come face to face with Mr Balloon Head.

"Are you home yet?" asked Demelza.

"I have arrived," said the pickled knight, "and am currently…" he paused and rolled his eyes back into his head, "heading over to clean the mountain of goose droppings from inside the wooden castle on the crazy golf course."

Honk! Captain Honkers shook his tail feathers.

"That's Honkers favourite place to go," said Demelza.

132

"You can tell what your body is doing, even though you're not, er, on it?" asked Jack.

"It is a skill I am developing," said the pickled knight, blinking hard. "But it does give me quite the headache!"

Kruawr-Kruawr-Kruawr!

As they rounded the cliffs, hundreds of black and white birds stared down at them from the entrances to their burrows in the rockface.

"That's A LOT of puffins!" Nessa stopped rowing for a minute to stare up at the noisy, white streaked cliffs. The pickled knight hopped down from the bow as puffins swooped overhead, some winging their way out to sea, others travelling back to their family burrows, bills filled with little fish.

Captain Honkers stayed low in the boat squeezed up against the pickled knight. Together, the two of them kept a wary eye on the swooping puffins. Demelza clutched her directions and guided Nessa and Jack towards the smallest cave entrance. She shivered as the boat finally slipped into the cave. Would they reach the cavern in time, or were they rowing straight into the lair of five ferocious, and very awake, giants? The noise of the waves and the puffins faded away, leaving only a distant roar and the creaking and splashing of the oars as they rowed deeper and deeper into the dark unknown.

Chapter Fourteen
PISKIES

Demelza's head torch beamed through the long narrow tunnels glinting off the slimy seaweed covered walls. She had been into caves near the beach before, but never the sea caves. You could only get to these caves by boat. In rough weather, when the tide rushed right the way in, seawater would blast up out of a spout-hole high up in the clifftops, like a whale's blowhole. She had been to see it with her mum and dad years ago, but it didn't seem nearly so much fun to think about from down here. Sailing into the caves, when the tide was still coming in, was dafter than a giraffe on stilts, but it wasn't as if they had a choice. Penfurzy depended on them!

She attached a second head torch to the pickled knight and plonked him back at the bow to light the way ahead, then settled at the stern to look at her map and directions.

She pointed at a clump of stalactites hanging from the roof.

"There's another tunnel just after those spiky cave teeth, be ready to turn…" she took a sneaky look at the letters she had drawn on the backs of her hands, "left! Now, now, now!" She grabbed a third broken oar from the bottom of the boat and wedged it in the mouth of the tunnel to keep them in place. Jack and Nessa fought to turn the boat until the bow finally rounded the corner. The current eased and Jack and Nessa were able to row down the new tunnel. It was much narrow than the last and they had to be careful not to keep knocking the oars on the rock walls.

"I can't imagine how Ren will feel if this works," Jack sighed. "I love her like she's my own sister, but she's sad a lot of the time. I can hear it when she sings. I wish she could go home. I wish we could stop travelling so much. But the world needs us to keep doing what we're doing, even if we're the only ones who know we're doing it.

"It'll work," said Nessa. "It has to."

The tunnel was getting narrower. Too narrow. Before long there was very little room left to row. They nudged the boat forward by pushing their way along the walls with the oars. The water was rising with the tide and they were taking too long.

"I've got an idea," said Nessa. "I went on a riverboat holiday with Mum and Dad a couple of years ago. "In really narrow tunnels, they did this." She lay on her back on one of the wooden benches and put her feet up on the rock wall. "Come on!"

Demelza lay on the bench behind Nessa, so that the tops of their heads were touching, and placed her feet up on the opposite wall. Jack lay on the other bench and propped his feet up.

"OK," Nessa pushed her feet into the wall with a grunt, "let's, umpfh! Get… argh, walking!"

Demelza and Jack copied Nessa, gripping the benches below them and pushing their feet hard against the tunnel wall until the boat began to move forwards.

"We're walking on the wall!" said Demelza as they walked the boat through the tunnel. "Just like spiders!"

"I wish we had as many legs," grunted Jack, "I don't like how fast the water is rising."

Demelza didn't either, the roof of the tunnel was getting far too close to her nose. If it rose much higher they would be crushed.

"How much further?" she squeaked.

The pickled knight looked at Demelza's map and shone his torch into the tunnel.

"I see the cavern, barely five rods ahead," he called back.

"Five what?" panted Demelza, her legs starting to ache as they picked up the pace.

"Five rods!" called the pickled knight, "Around twenty-seven yards."

"Yards?" grunted Nessa, "What's that in metres?"

"Metres?" called the pickled knight. "What is a metre?"

"Dad uses yards," panted Jack. "A yard is just under a metre, so I guess twenty seven yards is, urngh, just over, phew, twenty four metre... oh, never mind, we're here."

Their legs all flopped down over the edge of the boat as they floated out of the tunnel and into a little cave. They lay there for a minute as they caught their breath and waited for the feeling to come back into their legs. Tortuga bobbed on the water as they stared at the cave roof above. There was a hole in it.

Honk! Captain Honkers flapped excitedly as his honk bounced around the cave as if it were full of geese.

Honk-honk-hoooooonk!

"Stop that, feather brain," snapped the pickled knight as their ears were assaulted by a swarm of wild honks, "what now? Our exit is cut off. We must move quickly."

Demelza sat up. He was right. The tunnel they had come through was almost underwater already and the cave ceiling was getting closer all the time. She reached for her notes.

"That hole above us is where the water squeezes through to the blow-spout up on the cliffs. We need to get up there. Then we call for the piskies."

Jack made a sling with his hands and gave Demelza and Nessa a bunk up through the hole, then passed the pickled knight and

Captain Honkers up after them. By the time it was his turn the boat was high enough in the water for him to climb through with only a little help from the girls.

"It's lucky the tide is coming in," he said, "or we'd never have been able to get up here. I don't like how fast the water is rising though." He peered down through the hole as Tortuga bobbed closer and closer to the roof of the cave. "How do we call these piskies?"

"With a song," Demelza licked her finger and flicked through the pages of a notebook her mum had filled with notes and pictures of Penfurzy's magical creatures.

"I wish I hadn't asked," groaned Jack.

"Don't worry," said Demelza, "you don't have to sing. Nessa an' me wrote a piskie calling song this morning. But first, turn your coat inside out." She took off her anorak, turned the sleeves inside out and put it back on. "Mum's notes say it stops you getting piskie led." She waited as Jack and Nessa did the same. "They love to get people lost, but this will stop them messing with us." Nessa was wearing a body warmer over her denim jacket, so she turned that inside out too, just to be sure.

Nessa pulled her boombox out of the boat and switched it on. The cave filled with a bouncy beat. Demelza swallowed and gave Jack a shy grin as she began to rap, alternating lines with Nessa.

"Ready DJ Ness?"

"Ready here, D. All o' y'all piskies better listen to me."

"We rowed up in here, looking for a cave."

"A spriggan said you'd help us, it's time to be brave!"

"So come on out, piskies. Open up the way."

"Guide us to the giants, this ain't no time to play."

Play-ay-ay-ay. The end of the rap echoed around the cave, leaving only the beat from the boombox as they waited for a response.

"Do you think they heard?" whispered Jack.

"They heard," said Nessa as the wall began to open up behind him, revealing a dark narrow tunnel filled with dozens of tiny pairs of eyes, blinking in the light of their torches.

"Piskies!" said Demelza, as tiny little people dressed in rags and acorn hats marched out of the tunnel clapping their hands and stomping their feet to the beat.

"Awwwwww!" the piskies all groaned as Nessa turned off her boombox.

"Sorry guys, gotta save my battery power for the giants." The little people stopped dancing and shuffled closer together at the mention of giants. "Can you lead us to them?" The piskies nodded.

"Thanks," said Demelza. "We'd better go quickly."

The piskies didn't move, except to snarl at Captain Honkers as he nudged one with his beak and tried to decide if piskies might be as tasty as eyeballs.

"Naughty Honkers," Demelza picked him up. "Can we go now?" The piskies didn't seem any closer to moving. They prodded a slightly larger piskie forward. She was wearing a sparkly engagement ring on her head like a crown. She beckoned them down to her level and held out her hands as if she expected something.

There was a clunk from below as the boat hit the top of the cave and a glug-glug-glug as it filled with water.

"There she goes. Farewell, Tortuga," said Nessa sadly. "No way back."

"What are they waiting for?" asked Jack. "We need to go now!"

"Oh! I nearly forgot!" The piskies gathered around Demelza as she opened her bag. "Mum's notes said they like gifts of clothes. I got these from the toys in the lost property box at the caravan park." She pulled out a bundle of doll clothes. The piskies squealed in delight and scrambled over each other to grab them from her hands, squabbling among each other and dancing excitedly as they pulled on tiny flowery dresses, dungarees, fairy wings, a pink floppy hat with strawberries on it, an orange jumpsuit with a white helmet and yellow visor, ballet tutus, plastic Viking armour, camouflage jackets and trousers.

"Nice one, D," said Nessa as the piskies danced and twirled, in their strange, mismatched outfits. The piskie with the diamond crown waved to the group to follow them. "This is it." Nessa strapped her boombox over her shoulder and followed the group into the narrow tunnel which sloped gently downward.

The piskies moved quickly for their size, leaping, scrambling and dancing through the rocky tunnels, darting into crevices that Demelza couldn't even see until they followed the piskies into them and found new tunnels heading further and further into the heart of the island. By the giggling and whispering between them,

Demelza could tell that the piskies were finding it hard not to give in to the urge to lead them astray, as they did to travellers they found out on the moors and hills on misty nights. The pickled knight bounced ahead after the little creatures, snapping his yellow teeth and growling whenever he suspected they might be up to mischief. Demelza hoped the reversed jackets and angry head would be enough to keep them on the path.

"How are we going to find our way back?" Nessa whispered as they scrambled up over a ledge the piskies had leapt onto like circus fleas. Demelza was wondering the same thing. She couldn't imagine the piskies sticking around once they reached the giants, and there was no way they could get all the way back through the tunnels alone. But was there any point now that their boat had sunk?

"I guess that's a problem for later," said Jack as they sucked in their stomachs and wriggled through a narrow tunnel after the piskies, who were much quieter now. They communicated only in tiny whispers as they tiptoed forward, casting long shadows dancing in front of them in the torch light. Then, suddenly, they were gone.

"Where are they?" Demelza span around to shine her torch in all the nooks and crannies. There was no sign of the piskies. They were on their own.

"It's OK," said Jack. "We don't need them anymore."

"How do you know?" asked Nessa, before clapping her hand to her mouth and the other arm to her stomach. Demelza opened her mouth to speak, then shut it immediately as a terrible stench rolled down the tunnel. It wriggled up her nostrils and made her stomach burble in disgust. It was so bad she could taste it, a filthy mix of ancient cheesy socks, rotten eggs and dirty toilets.

"That's them. The giants." Jack pulled his bandana down and over his mouth and nose as they tiptoed out of the tunnel and into a cavern. "We're here."

Chapter Fifteen
THE PENFURZY GIANTS

Demelza couldn't see far in any direction, but from the feeling of the air and the change in how their footsteps sounded, it was clear that the cavern was enormous, like a vast cathedral. The smell was unbearable, even in this gigantic space. She wrapped a scarf around the bottom half of her face and tried to breathe as little as possible. Nessa had stuffed a wad of tissue up each nostril and pulled the neck of her t-shirt up over her mouth. Captain Honkers was staying very quiet and very close to Demelza. The only person who wasn't suffering from the smell was the pickled knight. Nessa switched off his headtorch and he hopped off into the darkness to explore.

Squelch-squelch-squelch

Demelza wrapped a nearly clean hanky around her torch to dim the light.

"Where are they?" she whispered to Jack as they crept through the stinking darkness. Jack didn't answer, he threw out his arm to stop them going any further.

"Look, there's something I need to tell you."

"About the giants?" asked Demelza, peering into the gloom to see if she could see them. Surely they should see something by now.

Jack rubbed the back of his neck. "Before we go any further, there's something I've got to tell you. I'm…"

"A liar!" growled the pickled knight, squelching back into their midst. "This varlet, this scoundrel has lied to us all. There are no giants here."

Demelza and Nessa stared at Jack, stepping back and pulling away from him as he lurched forward to grasp their hands.

"That's not true," he said as Nessa held out her palm, warning him not to come any closer.

"The truth?" shouted the pickled knight. "Come, see the truth for yourselves!"

"Wait!" hissed Jack, chasing after them as they ran after the bouncing head. "I can explain! Please! You've got to be quiet!"

"Behold!" announced the pickled knight as they reached the centre of the vast cavern. Four sleeping bodies lay on large stone slabs. Two men and two women. They were far from well-groomed with long straggly hair and beards, even the women had more hair hanging from their noses and chins than Demelza had on her head, and she had A LOT of hair on her head. They were larger than average humans, by maybe a foot or so, but they certainly couldn't be called giants. They smelled bad, like blue cheese that had been left out in the sun, but they didn't seem to be the source of the unbearable pong they had first smelled in the cavern.

"What's the deal, Jack?" Nessa narrowed her eyes and gave him her best cold hard stare. "You lied to us. Who are they, and why are you keeping them down here?"

"Get away from them," hissed Jack, grabbing their arms and trying to pull them away. "I'll tell you, but please, get away from them."

Demelza pulled out her foam sword and whacked Jack's arm until he let go. She kept it pointed at him as they moved away from the sleepers and crouched down behind a large flat rock.

"Talk," Demelza kept her sword pointed at his neck.

"Yes, talk, scoundrel!" barked the pickled knight. He bounced up onto the rock so that he could glare down at Jack. "Tell us the truth or die by the sword of a true Penfurzy knight!"

Demelza's sword bent in the middle as she pressed the tip against Jack's chin.

"Quiet! I'm trying to!" Jack stepped back from the sword and turned his eyes away from Nessa's sharp stare. "I know it looks like I'm lying, but they're not what they seem. They really are... oh no!" He stood up and ran his hand over the flat smooth rock the pickled knight was perched on. Demelza noticed it looked the same at the slabs the other people were lying on. Hadn't Jack said there were five giants? A distant sound was echoing through the cavern, growing louder and louder...

Honk-*HONK*-*HONK*-*HONK*
HOONNNK!

Captain Honkers came flapping out of the darkness like a white ghost. Feathers whirled behind him as he honked down at them, eyes wild with fear.

"Shush, Honkers! Please, shush!" Jack hissed, knocking Nessa over as he leapt up and waved his arms at the goose.

"Ow!" yelled Nessa as she fell back onto her boombox which scattered batteries across the dark uneven ground.

"Sorry!" Jack dropped to the floor next to her and began searching the rock with his hands. "The batteries, quick, collect them, we need to use Ren's song."

"What's wrong, Honkers?" asked Demelza as the goose dropped into her arms and tucked his head into her armpit. She had never seen him act like this before. Honkers wasn't afraid of anything, except maybe Jack's goose, Ellie. She listened to the darkness. Something stirred far in the distant depths of the vast cavern.

"Why do we need my boombox?" said Nessa, pushing Jack out of her way as he scrambled around her. "There are NO GIANTS, Jack. Who are these people, and why are you keeping them prisoner? Back off!" she pushed him away and snatched up the battery he was reaching for. "Say I believe Ren's song will keep them asleep, how do we know you're not going to trap us here too, now that we know all you're up to something?"

"Shush!" Demelza dropped Captain Honkers and knelt between them, her hands over their mouths.

"Listen!"

A distant pounding noise drew closer, and closer.

Boom-Boom-Boom!

Jack gripped Demelza's shoulder and shook her hand off his mouth. "It's too late. Please…" he gripped their shoulders, his green eyes wide and afraid, yet determined, "trust me, and fix that boombox!" He stood up and faced the darkness. The ground began to shake under their feet.

Boom-BOOM-BOOM!

"What are you going to do?" asked Demelza. Jack took a deep breath.

"I'll keep it away from you while you get the boombox working," said Jack. "When it's ready, get it to the centre of the circle and hit PLAY. Don't worry about me, OK? No matter what." He smiled nervously as he backed away into the darkness.

BOOM-BOOM-BOOM

"No matter what, OK? Just play the song!" he called as he turned and ran into the shadows.

Demelza and Nessa looked at each other, mouths open.

"Did he just leave us to get squished?" whispered Nessa.

BOOM-BOOM-BOOM!

"Giant!" screamed the pickled knight, leaping into Demelza's arms. **"GIANT!"**

HONK! Captain Honkers ran around them in circles, wings held wide as he honked at them to do something. Demelza and Nessa clutched each other to steady themselves, the whole world shook as a foot the size of a car stomped down out of the darkness. The pickled knight stopped shouting. Captain Honkers stopped honking. All was silent. They stared at the foot. Its smallest nail was as big as a bike wheel. It was so close they could see there was enough dirt under it to pot several plants. The stink was so bad their eyes began streaming. Demelza had to fight the urge to puke. The foot led to an ankle, then a leg as thick as a giant redwood tree, with hairs as thick as cables. The leg disappeared into ragged trousers which faded into the darkness as they huddled together, hoping that the giant couldn't see them way down here in the dark.

It sniffed.

It sniffed again. Then came a deep, rumbling woman's voice, cracked, as though coming from a dry throat after many years of sleep, **"Fe fi fo fum"**

A huge hand smacked down onto the ground only meters away. The whole cavern shook. Long strands of straggly hair swung down like long, dirty snakes, hanging from a head they could barely see. Demelza and Nessa were rooted to the floor of the cave, their legs wobbly and useless as they wriggled silently away from the searching fingers. All Demelza could think, as she stared at the hand, was how they could all be pancakes, right now, under there. Splatty, gooey pancakes, with crunchy bone bits. Why had Jack left them?

"Here, gigantor! Over here!"

Jack's voice called from the distance. Squinting through the gloom Demelza saw a light waving in the air. The giant had seen it too. Jack had turned on his torch and was waving it around, yelling to the giant. His voice was loud, not as loud as the giant's, but it wasn't his normal voice, it was deep and slower.

The hand stopped its blind search as the giant slowly registered the voice and movement in the distance. Demelza held her breath. The hand finally lifted and the huge feet pounded away, towards Jack.

BOOM-BOOM-BOOM

Demelza switched on her dimmed headtorch and scrambled around with Nessa for the batteries as Jack's voice and running footsteps sounded in the darkness, followed by the giant's thundering footsteps as it lumbered blindly after him.

"I've got three!" Demelza shoved the great big batteries into the back of the boombox then lay down and slid her arms around to find more. "How many are there?"

"Ten!" Nessa shoved another two in after the others. "There are seven in here, three to go."

"Mmpfh!" The pickled knight bounced over and spat one into Nessa's hand.

"Ack, thanks!" Nessa wiped it on her jeans and pounced on another battery Captain Honkers had sent rolling with his flapping feet. "One more, D!"

Running footsteps drew closer, followed by the giant's thundering feet as she charged in the direction of Jack's voice, calling from the other side of the cave. Demelza wondered how he could run so fast, and how long he could keep on going as her fingers closed triumphantly on the last battery. Nessa shoved it into the boombox and snapped the cover closed.

"Showtime!" They ran with the boombox to the centre of the circle of sleeping figures. Only they weren't so fast asleep now. The eyes of the older two were blinking awake as they stirred.

"Are we sure about this, D?" said Nessa. "I know there's one giant out there, but we don't know who these people are, or why Jack's people are keeping them here."

The footsteps grew louder again. Demelza's heart flapped around in her chest like Captain Honkers wings as she wondered what to do. She trusted Jack, didn't she? She thought about his kind eyes and easy smile and remembered her mum's letter, Listen to your heart.

"I'm sure," said Demelza. "I trust him. Let's do it."

Nessa held the boombox up as the figures began to stretch and groan. Demelza whacked the volume sliders to full and hit PLAY.

Nothing happened.

Demelza pressed rewind, but it did nothing. The boombox was dead and the four figures around them weren't just waking up, they were growing up. Very, very far up. They were surrounded. By giants.

Chapter Sixteen
SONG OF THE SEA

The giants were still half asleep, rubbing their eyes as they stretched and clambered to their feet. They hadn't seen the girls yet. Nessa and Demelza danced out of their way as they lumbered around, growing bigger every second. Jack's voice called out of the darkness,

"Over here, cheese toes!"

Demelza clutched at Nessa. He didn't know the others were awake! she willed him to be quiet with all her might, but it was too late, the giants stumbled in the direction of his voice. Jack suddenly went quiet. He must have heard their footsteps. Or had the first giant caught him and crunched him up, bones and all? They had to help, but how could they without the boombox? Without Ren's song?

HONK-HONK-HOOOOOONK!

Captain Honkers flapped off into the darkness. Demelza bit her tongue to stop herself screaming for him to come back. Honkers may have been a goose, but he always knew what he was doing.

HONK-HONK-HOOOOOONK!

He honked as he flew through the cavern, leading the giants away from where they had last heard Jack's voice calling from.

The thundering feet stopped as the giants' big, slow brains registered the new noise. They began to lumber in the direction of the honking. Captain Honkers kept up the racket as he swooped and dived around the cavern, keeping the giants well away from the girls. But what good was it? The boombox was dead. There was no way to stop them.

"Batteries!" Nessa smacked her forehead. She dropped to her knees and pulled open the compartment on the boombox. "D, did you check which way you put them in?"

"I... Er, no?" said Demelza. She wrung her hands as she listened out for Captain Honkers. His honks were growing quieter, he must be getting tired. Nessa emptied out the batteries and began slotting them back in. The pickled knight bounced up onto the slab next to Demelza.

"Switch on my torch!"

"Why?" she whispered. "The giants will see it."

"That, my dear imp, is the point!" he said in as noble a voice as he could manage.

Demelza gently fist-bumped his cheek and switched on his torch. He gave her a grin then leapt off the slab and away into the darkness, his light bobbing up and down as he hollered,

"For justice, for glory, for Penfuuuuurzeeee!"

The cavern shook with pounding feet as the giants ran after him, bashing their heads on the stalactites and sending them crashing to the ground.

"I need light here," said Nessa sorting through the batteries. Demelza knelt held her dimmed torch close to the boombox so that Nessa could see which direction each set of batteries should be facing.

Captain Honkers flew over to perch on one of the slabs as the pickled knight lured away the giants, giving him time to recover.

"Hurry," Demelza squeaked as she became aware of a padding noise behind her, like someone very, very big, trying to move very, very quietly.

"What's up?" came a loud whisper. A face the size of Demelza herself appeared above them. Captain Honkers leapt back into the air and flapped away, honking loudly. Demelza opened her mouth to scream but nothing came out.

"Jack?" squeaked Nessa as she almost dropped the boombox again, "You're a..."

"Giant. Yes. And no," said Giant Jack. "Mostly no, but no time to explain." Demelza stared at him. He was the same Jack, but the height of a house, which was much smaller than the other giants charging around the cavern, but still huge!

"What's the hold up?" he asked. Nessa finally found her voice.

"Batteries. Buh-batteries the wrong way around," she swallowed her questions, shoved the last few batteries into place and clipped the compartment shut. "Good to go now," she paused. "Will this affect you too?

Do you want to, you know…" she mimed putting her fingers in her ears. "I will. But it may not work, you need to play this full volume." Demelza began to stuff tissue into her own ears. "It's OK. You're safe," he smiled. "You're one hundred percent human, you'll be fine. Dad lied back at the marsh, so that you wouldn't realise what we are. Me and him."

"So, what are you?" asked Nessa.

"Later. Remember what I said, play the music. No matter what." He nodded to her and shoved his fingers into his dinner plate sized ears. Nessa climbed onto one of the slabs and held the boombox high. Demelza hit PLAY again. This time Ren's voice rang out through the cavern, loud, strong and very, very beautiful. As the song echoed around the cavern the pounding, shaking and roaring died down. The giants had stopped running. Captain Honkers swooped down into Demelza's arms. She hugged him tight, rubbing her cheek against his feathers in her relief to see him safe.

"Well done, sisters!" called the pickled knight as he bounced out of the shadows and up onto the slab with them. He gazed up at the boombox as Ren's incredible lullaby poured out, filling the cavern which amplified the volume until they could barely hear the giants' booming footsteps as they closed in. Jack remained kneeling by the slab, fingers firmly in his ears, though Demelza could tell the song was getting through, his eyelids were drooping and she could swear he was starting to shrink ever so slowly.

"You hear that?" said Nessa, her mouth right against Demelza's ear so that she could be heard. "The footsteps are getting softer, I think they're shrinking."

"I hope they do it fast," said Demelza, "because here they come!"

The headtorches revealed huge figures looming out of the dark. They were still human shaped, but hunched and troll-like in their giant form. Their bloodshot eyes rolled wildly around under thick eyebrows, their lips were flecked with foam and strings of drool that dripped down to the ground creating gooey puddles. The smell of them was overpowering. Demelza buried her nose in Captain Honker's feathers as Nessa tried to hold her breath.

The giants seemed dazed, lulled by Ren's song, but their boulder sized fists were clenched tightly, swinging by their sides as they searched for the source of the sound.

"Their eyesight isn't good," said Demelza. She took off the pickled knight's head torch and threw it into the centre of the circle. The giants paused and snarled as they followed the movement.

BOOM!

A huge fist pounded down, smashing the torch to pieces and leaving only the dull glow of Demelza's torch under her hankie. She didn't dare turn it off and leave them in complete darkness.

"Get down," Jack mouthed to them, his head rolling as he fought a yawn. He was shrinking fast. The giants were shrinking too, but they were still the height of double decker busses. Their fists rained down, pounding the slabs and the ground, sending Captain Honkers squawking up into the air. The giants didn't chase him, their twitching nostrils showed they were looking for something else.

"Fe fi fo fum"

they all growled. Demelza took Nessa's arm and helped her down from the slab so that she could keep tight hold of the blaring boombox. Ren's song was working, they were tiring, but one wrong move and they could still be splatted.

"Fe fi fo fum"

"They really say that?" Nessa murmured. "Cheesy!"

"It's ancient Gaelic," said Demelza as they ducked to avoid a grasping hand just above their heads. "When she read Jack and the Beanstalk Mum told me it means something like, Food. Good for eating. Enough for my hunger."

"Oh," Nessa went quiet and yanked her foot back as the growing pool of giant drool reached her trainers. "Now I kinda wish it was just a cheesy fairy-tale quote."

Something was happening to the tape. Ren's voice was getting slower and deeper.

"The batteries," Nessa hissed as they stepped back over "They're nearly out of juice."

Demelza looked up at the giants. They were moving slowly now, hands only half-heartedly swatting and grasping the air.

Their eyelids drooped and huge yawns released damp eggy smelling yawns. They were now only three times Demelza's height now, but even half asleep, they still looked dangerous. As Ren's voice slowed a little more they seemed to be fighting the song – fighting to stay awake. Jack was normal sized now, and lying on the cave floor, eyes half closed. Demelza wondered for one second if they should stop the tape, but Jack seemed to know what she was thinking and shook his head. No matter what, he had said.

"Help me," Nessa whispered in her ear. She opened the battery compartment, took off her fingerless gloves and began rubbing the batteries. Demelza dropped to her knees to join in. They did this whenever the batteries in their torches or walkie talkies ran low. She put her palms over the batteries and began rubbing too. It wouldn't do much, but warmth helped batteries conduct just a tiny bit better. Maybe it would make them last juuuust long enough. Nessa turned the volume down a little, they didn't need it quite so loud with all of the giants gathered here. Ren's voice picked up a little, reaching almost normal speed as the batteries warmed under their hands.

"It's working!" said Demelza as the smallest giant slumped over a slab and began to snore. The others sank to their knees, then down to the floor, and not a second too soon. With the last bit of juice in the batteries spent, the boombox faded into silence. The only sounds now was rumbling snores and the squelch-squelch-squelch of the pickled knight hopping from one giant to another to make sure they were asleep.

Nessa sat back and sighed with relief. She clenched her knuckles for a weary fist bump from Demelza.

They switched on their torches to see five large sleeping bodies slumped around the circle. Jack was sleeping just as soundly. Demelza shook his shoulder hard, but he didn't react at all.

"Do you think Ren can wake him up?" said Demelza, lifting up his eyelids and shining her torch into his eyes. "We could make some kind of stretcher from our coats and some sticks to drag him out on."

"Maybe."

Demelza didn't like Nessa's tone. It sounded as if there was a "but" coming.

"But... where's the way out, D? How can we take him with us if we're stuck here?"

Demelza took Nessa's torch and shone it around, its super strong beam almost reaching even the furthest walls. There was no sign of the way they had come in. The piskies has sealed the tunnel behind them. The only other way in was the tunnel that led to the quarry, and even if they found it stupid Connan's firework display had sealed it shut. Nessa was right. There was no way out.

Chapter Seventeen
CAN ANY BODY HELP?

Demelza's footsteps echoed in her ears as she ran around the huge cavern searching for a way out, no matter how tiny. Captain Honkers ran next to her, flapping his wings and honking in a concerned tone as he tried to keep up. Demelza had tried to send him off to search for a way he could escape on his own and bring help, maybe a tunnel way up in the cavern roof, but he wouldn't leave her side. Not when his dear, featherless mum looked so worried.

The dome shape of this section carried sound well and she could hear Nessa's voice and the squelch-squelch-squelch of the pickled knight as they searched along the far wall.

"Let's take a break," called Nessa at last. "Meet you in the middle!"

Demelza sighed and dragged her heavy legs back to where the giants slept. She pulled an apple juicebox out of her bag, slurped half of it and handed it to Nessa who drained the rest. They froze and stared at each other as they realised they had guzzled the only drink they had with them.

"It's OK," said Nessa, putting her hand on Demelza's arm as she rifled through her bag and laid out their remaining rations: a chocolate bar, two packets of crisps, two slightly bruised apples and one squishy banana covered in brown swirling patterns she had drawn with a blunt pencil when bored.

"D!" Nessa shook her shoulders and looked into her eyes. "Don't worry. We'll make it out. We'll be OK, we always are."

Nessa's calmness in the face of disaster always helped Demelza feel better when she was frightened, but not this time. She shook off Nessa's hands.

"That's a daft thing to say. Don't you ever get worried? Just because we've got out of stuff before doesn't mean everything will always work out, OK?"

"Sorry, D," said Nessa, her eyes concerned. "It's not that I'm not taking this seriously. It's just… I trust us. All of us. We'll get out of this."

"Yeah, well," Demelza stared down at their rations through hot tears. "I bet Mum thought she'd be OK when she took a risk and tried to get out to Penfurzy Castle. But she wasn't, was she?" She pulled out her hanky and hid her face in it, wiping her eyes and nose. "She fell, and left me and Dad alone. We came out here without telling Dad and now he might be completely alone, forever." Her shoulders shook as a sob broke loose. Nessa put an arm around her. She tried to wriggle away but Nessa pulled her even closer and held her tight. Demelza gave in to the hug and buried her face in Nessa's jacket, breathing in the familiar smell of bubblegum and hair gel until the tears stopped and she managed to take a breath without it turning to shuddering sobs.

"I'm here, D. I'll always be here for you, and I know your mum is too. She helped us get here. We may be stuck for now, but we saved Penfurzy, again! Maybe the world. If, and that's a BIG if, we don't get out, at least we've saved people. A LOT of people. They're safe because of what we did here."

The pickled knight sniffed as a tear rolled down his cheek.

"That we have, brave knights! If only I could say one last fare thee well to Bod now that we are forever separated, again."

Demelza reached down and pulled the pickled knight and Captain Honkers into the shared hug.

"Wait, that's it!" said Nessa. She grabbed the pickled knight by the ears and planted a kiss on his forehead. "Your body! You can communicate with it, right?"

"Yes," said the pickled knight, one eyebrow raised.

"Then you can tell Demelza's dad we're trapped and give him directions to the cave. I bet Mr Greensplat will let him use his boat!"

"But how could he give Dad the message?" said Demelza. "His body can't speak without a head. Ohhhh, of course! He could write it down. Could you do that, Sir Calenick? Could you save us?"

The pickled knight shifted awkwardly on his neck stump and avoided looking either of them in the eye.

"In theory, yes. But, there is one problem," he turned away and stared at the floor. "I... I cannot read or write. I am sorry, my brave friends. I cannot do what you ask. My failure has doomed you to starve in these caves while my immortal bonce watches you turn to skeletons down here in the dark. Oh, alas and alack! Woe betide us all!"

"Hey, it's OK," said Demelza, gently. "It doesn't matter that you can't read or write. No one ever taught you. I guess it wasn't so important when you were alive."

"Well, no," sniffed the pickled knight. "It was more for religious types and the nobler nobles."

"See? And you don't even need to be able to read or write to get a message to Dad. All you need to do is copy what I write. Do you think you could do that?" The pickled knight held himself tall.

"I will throw my heart and soul into it!" he announced. "They're with my body right now, but they're ready to help."

"Great," Demelza grabbed one of the broken pieces of chalk that were always rolling around in her bag. "Can your body find a pen and a piece of paper? There are some in my caravan, if you're nearby?"

The pickled knight rolled his eyes up into his head.

"OK, I'm heading to your caravan. I'm getting the spare key from under the bottom step. I'm climbing... wait, no! I'm being attacked! The children from caravan four, they're throwing water-balloons at me!"

"Don't turn around!" shouted Demelza and Nessa at once, visions of terrified kids seeing a badly drawn face on a balloon instead of a head running through their minds.

"I'm not turning," said the pickled knight. "I am enduring the onslaught. I'm climbing the steps, I'm unlocking the door and, oh-oh-oh no! They've knocked the balloon out of my balaclava! It's floating away. They're screaming, they're running... they're gone."

Demelza cringed as she imagined what the boys would tell their parents.

"I am sitting at your desk with a crayon and paper," said the pickled knight. "I am ready to begin."

Demelza stuck her tongue out of the corner of her mouth and began to write on the ground in big careful letters that she hoped would be easy to copy:

Dear Dad,

The pickled knight looked hard at the shape of the letters, then rolled his eyes up again and stuck his own tongue out of the corner of his mouth as his body wrote them down at the little desk miles away in Demelza's caravan. It took a long time. The pickled knight had to concentrate very hard to make sure he was getting the letters right. Demelza wondered how he could be sure he wasn't just scrawling nonsense all over the table instead of the paper, but had to trust the strange connection the severed head had with its body. She paused as she got to the part where they had to call for the piskies.

"How do we know they'll appear for Dad?" she asked Nessa. "They closed the path behind them and left us here. What if they do the same again? Then Dad will be trapped too!"

"Don't worry about that," said Nessa. "Tell him to meet us where we left Tortuga. I'll deal with the piskies." They both put their hands on their hearts at the mention of their dear boat.

"May she rest in peace," they said in unison, heads bowed.

"OK, I have all that," said the pickled knight. "Anything else?"

"Just one more thing." Demelza scrawled carefully on the ground.

Pls bring snacks.
Luv, Melza

"Good thinking," Nessa stood up and brushed off her jeans as the pickled knight worked on the message. "Right, let's sort out these pesky piskies!" She grabbed a stick of broken stalactite and began rapping on the rock wall around the spot where they had entered.

"Hey-hey, piskies! The big dudes are sleeping again. Time to let us out." She tapped on the wall again, "I know you're there. You must have heard what went down in here."

Silence. There were no piskies to be seen or heard.

"Message delivered," called the pickled knight. He bounced over to join them. "My body posted the note through the letterbox then knocked and ran away."

"Did Dad read it?" asked Demelza

"I believe so. He was walking to the door as I retreated to my caravan. Wait a second," his eyes rolled up into his head. "Yes. He's running out of the house now. He's getting into the car aaaand, off he goes."

"It's no use him coming if we can't get to the meeting point," said Demelza. "The piskies won't open up and help us."

"Leave them to me!" growled the pickled knight. "Reveal yourselves, sprites! Open up and guide us to freedom or I'll hunt you down and crunch your bones and…"

"Whoa, fella!" Nessa nudged him with her foot. "Let's try debts before threats."

"What do you mean, debts?" asked Demelza. Nessa winked and rapped on the wall again.

"Word up, piskies! As I see it, you owe us. These giants would have cleared all the humans off this island. There would have been no one left to leave food, milk and gifts for you. No one to play tricks on. Soon enough you'd all have been squished into piskie pancakes. We saved you. Now it's your turn to save us."

Still no sound. The wall remained as solid as ever. Demelza took the stalactite and rapped the wall herself.

"Should I call my friend, the Great Spriggan of Penfurzy Tor?" she shouted. "Maybe he could convince you. Hellooooo! Mr Spriiiiiigaaaaan!"

Nessa and the pickled knight joined in the call.

"Mr Spriggan, Mr Spriggan, Mr Spriiiiiigaaaaan!"

Honk, Honk, HOOOOOOONK-Honk! honked Captain Honkers.

There was a loud magical crack. The wall opened in front of them and several hundred piskies tumbled out. They scrambled up Nessa and Demelza's legs, pleading to them to stop shouting.

"Shusssh!" they shouted, eyes wide with fear.

"Just a joke! We'll take you, we'll take you!" panted their leader as she clambered up to Demelza's shoulder.

"Oh, so you can speak human?" said Demelza.

"Come on!" the piskie looked around twitchily for any sign of the spriggan. "Let's go!"

Nessa held up her hand for a high five from Demelza.

"I guess in some cases, threats beat debts," she smiled.

Chapter Eighteen
JACK'S SECRET

The piskies jumped up and down, urging Nessa and Demelza to go with them. The pickled knight snapped his teeth as they scampered around him, pulling on his hair and beard, dragging him towards the tunnel.

"What about Jack?" asked Demelza, as the piskie leader tugged her hair and pleaded with her to hurry. The leader whistled and a stream of piskies swarmed towards the sleeping boy. Suddenly his body was floating over the floor, held aloft by hundreds of pairs of tiny hands.

"Wait!" shouted Nessa. She ran back to the sleeping giants, grabbed the arm of the smallest and began to pull and shove him onto the slab he was slumped over.

Demelza hurried over to help. She grabbed his other arm and helped Nessa drag him up until he was lying on his back on the slab. The smell was easier to bear now that they were almost human size. The pong seemed to increase as they grew.

"What are you doing?" asked the leader, jumping nervously from foot to foot on Demelza's shoulder. She fought through Demelza's hair to shout into her ear. "They would have crunched you up, bones and all. They're already asleep. Why are you making them comfortable?"

"Because it's the least we can do," said Nessa. "They were here before us. Then humans hunted and killed them. Now we're making them sleep below ground, as if we're the most important creatures on the planet. Like I said, it's the least we can do."

The piskie leader sighed and whistled to her tribe. They swarmed over to the giants who, with the help of many tiny hands, began to magically slither up into comfortable positions on the slabs. Demelza marvelled at the strength of the tiny piskies, each one lifting many, many times its own body weight. People had laughed at old Merrin Carnkie when she told everyone in Ms Bocaddon's café that she had seen a surprised and rather dizzy cow being carried round in circles by four piskies, one under each hoof. Now Demelza believed she had been telling the truth.

With the giants back in place, Nessa grabbed her boombox and they all hurried after the piskies. Captain Honkers and the pickled knight rode on Jack's body, which looked like a very weird giant caterpillar with hundreds of piskie legs scurrying beneath him. The sleeping Jackerpillar scuttled over rocks and down uneven slopes as his two passengers rode him like a surfboard.

"Do you think your dad will be there?" asked Nessa as they approached the chamber above the cave where Tortuga had sunk.

"He will," said Demelza. She knew it in her heart. "He's always there for me. Even when I don't know I want him to be. He won't let us down."

Nessa squeezed Demelza's hand as they ducked down to squeeze into the chamber below the clifftop spout-hole. The Jackerpillar scurried after them. The piskies laid Jack gently on the floor and streamed away, back into the tunnel. Their leader tugged on a curl of Demelza's hair.

"Our debt is paid," she said. "You will tell the spriggan that we guided you well?"

"We will," said Demelza. "Thank you."

The piskie gave them a curt nod, then clambered down Demelza's back to follow her people into the tunnels. The entrance faded back into solid rock behind them. Nessa and Demelza lay on the damp floor and looked down through the hole into the chamber below.

The tide had gone out leaving the water level much lower. A few pieces of wood bobbed on the surface, all that remained of Tortuga.

"No sign of him yet."

"Give him time," said Demelza. "He'll be here." She chewed her nails as she wondered whether there was time for him to get a boat and row out here before the tide came back in. An eerie moan filled the cavern and chilled her bones.

"It's OK," said Nessa. "It's the wind blowing over the spout-hole, like panpipes."

Demelza looked up at the very distant glimmer of grey sky through the spout-hole high up in the forbidden cliffs. It sounded as though the storm was picking up. Nessa was a brilliant climber, but Demelza knew there was no way even she could climb that smooth, slimy vertical tunnel, especially with rain drizzling down the walls. She wondered for a second whether they would survive being blasted out of the spout in a jet of water if the tide did rush in, but decided quickly that it wouldn't be nearly as much fun as she pictured it. She sat cross-legged with Captain Honkers on her lap and shared out the rest of the snacks in her backpack. As they ate in silence, listening for the tell-tale sound of oars in the cavern below, Demelza finally said what had been on her mind for a while.

"So, your fibs…"

Nessa's eyebrow raised.

"Fibs?"

"Fibs. You've stopped telling fibs."

"What are you talking about? I don't tell fibs."

"Ooh, what a fib!" chuckled the pickled knight bobbing around on his neck stump as he enjoyed the awkward conversation.

"I don't mind," Demelza shuffled closer to Nessa and nudged her shoulder with her own. "I love your stories, but you know… I never reeeeally believed you were a pirate captain, or a spy, or a circus ringleader, or a ninja."

Nessa's cheeks tinged a tiny bit pink in the dimly lit chamber.

"But, I do know that you could be any of those things. Y'know, if you wanted to, 'cos you're brilliant. And brave. And the bestest friend I could have in the whole wide world."

Nessa blushed even harder and leaned into Demelza's shoulder.

"OK, maybe I sometimes exaggerated the truth a teeeeny bit…"

"Aha, another fib!" cackled the pickled knight, then pressed his lips tightly together at a stern glance from Demelza.

"But," continued Nessa, "that's 'cos life was always boring. I didn't have many people to hang out with. Well, not people I could be myself with. People like you, Honkers, even Pickles there." She picked at the stripes on her trainers. "It's just, life is different now. I guess, the amazing things we've seen and done together are better than anything I could make up." She smiled and nudged Demelza with her shoulder. "I don't have to pretend anymore. Life is amazing. So are you, D."

Demelza beamed to herself in the dark. She remembered what it had been like on Penfurzy before Nessa had shown up. Lonely, grey and dull, even with all her pretend adventures with Captain Honkers. Now she realised Penfurzy had always been full of mystery and adventure, just as her mum had known. Mysteries that had scared Demelza's dad when her mum had died on one of her quests. Scared him into hiding away her notebooks in case Demelza followed in her footsteps. But all that had changed when Nessa had arrived. He had even opened up the box of notebooks again after they had found the lost Penfurzy Castle and saved Demelza's home. She put her hand in her pocket and clutched her mother's letter and promised herself that they would solve every mystery in her notebooks.

"You're amazinger," Demelza smiled. She tucked her arm through the crook of Nessa's elbow and they sat there, leaning into each other for warmth as the wind whistled above them.

A distant splash echoed up through the chamber.

"Dad?" Demelza and Nessa scrambled to the hole in the floor and stuck their heads through. Demelza strained her ears for the sound of a wooden boat or oars knocking on the wall of the narrow tunnel they had walked their boat along. There was only a gentle splash-splashing, then… a voice. A slightly grumbly voice complaining about sea caves not being what they used to be.

"Mr Greensplat!" shouted Nessa.

"Demelzaaaa!"

"DAD!" Demelza yelled as his deep comforting voice called out her name. **"DAAAAD! Up here!"** A rubber dingy floated out of the tunnel and into the cavern. Mr Greensplat held up his lantern and Demelza's dad's jaw dropped to see four arms waving from a hole in the cave roof.

"Demelza? Nessa! What in Penfurzy are you doing up there? No, don't tell me. We'll have a LONG conversation about that later, once you're home safe."

Demelza knew that tone of voice. It would be a very long conversation, followed by weeks and weeks of extremely good behaviour and lots of extra jobs to do in the house and caravan park, but it was all worth it.

"Um, Dad…" before we come down… our friend Jack is up here. He's asleep, so we'll have to help him down to you."

"Asleep? Asleep!" shouted Mr Greensplat "Then wake the lad up!"

"It's not a normal sleep," called Nessa. "We can't wake him up. But don't worry. We know someone who can help him."

"Demelza?" called her dad, "What happened to Jack? Did he have an accident?"

"No, he's really just asleep," called Demelza through the hole. "He'll be OK, Dad, honest!" Her dad sighed and reached up with his big strong arms. Demelza and Nessa gently moved Jack over to the hole. They each grabbed him under an armpit and lowered him down into the waiting hands of Demelza's dad and Mr Greensplat.

Demelza went next, clambering down until she was hanging from her fingers then dropping down into her dad's arms and giving him the biggest, squeeziest hug she had ever given anyone. There was a scuffling noise above, like the sound of a reluctant severed head being shoved into a rucksack, then Nessa lowered herself down into the boat. A very happy Captain Honkers dropped down onto Mr Greensplat's head then flapped excitedly around Demelza's dad as he laid Jack out in the bottom of the boat.

"That's no normal sleep," muttered Mr Greensplat, lifting one of Jack's eyelids. "He's under a spell. A strong one at that. What happened to him?"

"It's a long story," said Demelza, wondering how she would even explain it. "We've got to get him back to the fairground."

"No, we've got to get him to a hospital," said her dad.

"Please," Demelza grabbed her dad's hand and looked him in the eyes. "Trust me, we need to get him back to fairground. There's someone there who can help him."

Her dad paused. Demelza put her hand on his and made her eyes as big as possible.

"OK," said her dad with a sigh. "We'll take him there first." He nodded to Mr Greensplat as he handed out lifejackets. "Let's get out of here before that storm traps us."

Demelza and Nessa sat in the back of the boat, watching Jack's head roll gently from side to side as Demelza's dad and Mr Greensplat guided the boat through the huge system of tunnels. Demelza held tightly to the thought that Ren really would be able to wake Jack from his magical sleep.

"Mr Penrose," said Nessa, "you didn't sail all the way out here in this dinghy, did you?"

"Of course not!" scoffed Mr Greensplat as they finally rounded the corner into the cave that led out to the open sea, "this little thing would be thrown onto the rocks and we'd all be gull food if we tried that in this weather! We came in my little fishing boat. Anchored her right here in this cave, see…? Oh."

Mr Greensplat dropped to his knees. There was no boat waiting to take them to safety, just an empty cave and the stormy sea beyond.

Chapter Nineteen
MORVOREN

Demelza held onto one of the ropes on the side of the dingy as waves swept into the cave, sploshed up over the rocky walls then sucked back out to sea sending the little dinghy bobbing and swirling around the cave.

"Any ideas, Humfra?" Demelza's dad shouted over the thundering waves.

"Just one." Mr Greensplat shouted back. "Hold tight!"

They all dropped to the floor around Jack and thrust their arms through the rope that ran around the sides of the dinghy. They joined hands as the waves whipped the craft out of the cave and onto the open sea.

They bounced up and over wave after wave as they were carried further and further out to sea. Demelza bit her lip until it bled. Why did they make the pickled knight write that note? They should have stayed in the giant's cave rather than dooming her dad and Mr Greensplat to a terrible fate too. Now they were all going to be drowned, or eaten by sharks, or giant squid or…

"Morvoren!" shouted Mr Greensplat, his eyes wide.

"Morvoren?" Demelza raised her head as much as she could without letting go her grip of the rope and her dad and Nessa's hands.

"My boat, Morvoren!" She's coming back for us!"

Demelza blinked in the salty ocean spray. Through the mist she could just make out the shape of a little boat heading straight for them.

"Your boat is called Morvoren?"

"After the girl I loved and lost," sighed Mr Greensplat. "But at least my boat is returning to me from the sea, even if she never did."

"Who's sailing it?" Nessa asked. "And is it still called sailing if the sail has been ripped off?"

"Look lower," gasped Demelza. "At the water!"

In the frothing foam around the boat they caught flashes of scales and fins. And was that a dolphin, and a seal, and the long, spotted back of a whale shark? The boat was being carried to them by sea creatures.

Demelza's dad grabbed a rope and lashed the dingy to a metal ring on the side of the boat and lifted Demelza and Nessa up so that they could climb aboard. With Mr Greensplat's help, he gently lifted Jack up to lie on the deck next to them.

"Morvoren, my beautiful boat. I thought I'd lost you forever," said Mr Greensplat. He hugged the mast of the little craft and stroked the scraps of remaining sail gently, as though it were a broken wing.

Nessa nudged Demelza and pointed to a familiar figure with long flowing hair who was climbing aboard. She stood on the deck in front of them, long wavy hair flowing down to the deck as her fins transformed into feet.

"Ren! You're free!" shouted Demelza, "And you really are a mermaid!" She felt her cheeks flush with embarrassment the second she said it, but Ren gave her a gentle smile then walked towards Mr Greensplat. He was staring at her, hand raised to his open mouth.

"Mor… Morvoren?" he gasped. He staggered back as if his legs had turned to jelly then sat down hard, blinking as if he could hardly believe what he was seeing. "You're… how…?" Ren put her hands on his cheeks and brushed his forehead with her lips. Demelza could swear that he looked twenty years younger at her touch.

Demelza's dad was sitting quietly and nodding as he watched everything happening around him with glazed eyes. He had seen lots of strange things as a roadie with the band, Pontefract. He wasn't going to let a mermaid surprise him too much.

"Is he OK?" asked Demelza as Ren crouched by Jack and put her ear to his chest.

"He heard your song and fell asleep," said Nessa. "I guess you know he's a…" she cupped her hand around her mouth so that only Demelza and Ren could see her whisper, "giant."

"Not exactly a giant," said Ren. "But that's his story to tell, when he wakes."

"So, you can wake him?" said Demelza, relief flooding through her.

"Of course," said Ren. "With a song." She stroked Jack's forehead and began to sing. Nessa and Demelza shuffled back to sit between Demelza's dad and Mr Greensplat. The old fisherman hadn't taken his eyes off Ren since she stepped on board, but was unable to form any words that actually made sense. They all sat, entranced by Ren's beautiful singing as if they were bobbing in a bubble of calm on the raging sea. Jack began to stir as Ren sang. Demelza slid her fingers between Nessa's and laid her head on her dad's shoulder. Captain Honkers curled up contentedly in her lap.

Jack eyes opened as Ren finished her song. His eyebrows knitted together in confusion as he realised he was lying on a boat with Demelza's dad and Mr Greensplat staring at him.

"Did it work?" he asked.

"It worked," grinned Nessa. She clasped his hand and pulled him into a sitting position.

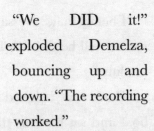

"We DID it!" exploded Demelza, bouncing up and down. "The recording worked."

"It worked," said Ren quietly. She glanced at Mr Greensplat, then Jack. "Then, I don't have to keep travelling? I could, maybe, stay here?"

"We'll talk to Dad," said Jack. "But, I guess, yes."

Mr Greensplat grasped Ren's hand. The two of them gazed at each other, holding a silent conversation with their eyes.

"Need a tow?" boomed a woman's voice over a loudhailer, breaking the spell.

"Mum!" gulped Nessa as a large boat chugged out of the sea fret to loom over them. "You called Mum?" she asked Demelza's dad as she waved nervously up at the woman leaning over the railing, feeding a tow line down to them.

"I heard that," Nessa's mum called through the loudhailer, "and just as well he did! We'll have a little chat about this when I'm not on duty."

"Can't wait," sighed Nessa as they attached the tow-line to the boat and sat back as the large lifeboat towed them to the closest cove , around the western cliff to the northern shore as the sinking sun winked at them from behind the cairn high on the tor. Demelza wondered if the spriggan knew they had succeeded in their quest. All was well on Penfurzy. All was safe. For now, at least.

Jack's parents and the fair folk were waiting as the boat pulled into a cove below the tor. A huge cheer went up as they raced down into the water to help pull the fishing boat ashore. Nessa's mum and her crew moored their own boat at the little jetty as they stared in surprise at the reception waiting for them.

Jack's mum, Rose, swept him up into her arms and raised an eyebrow. Jack nodded and his dad punched the air with a loud whoop as cheers and applause filled the air.

Demelza's dad still looked dazed as Jack's mum kissed him on both cheeks and Big Jack clapped him on the back. Nessa's mum received the same treatment as Demelza, Nessa and Jack were swept up onto shoulders and carried all the way back to the campsite behind the fairground like returning heroes. Mr Greensplat and Ren walked well behind the rest of the group, hand in hand and deep in conversation.

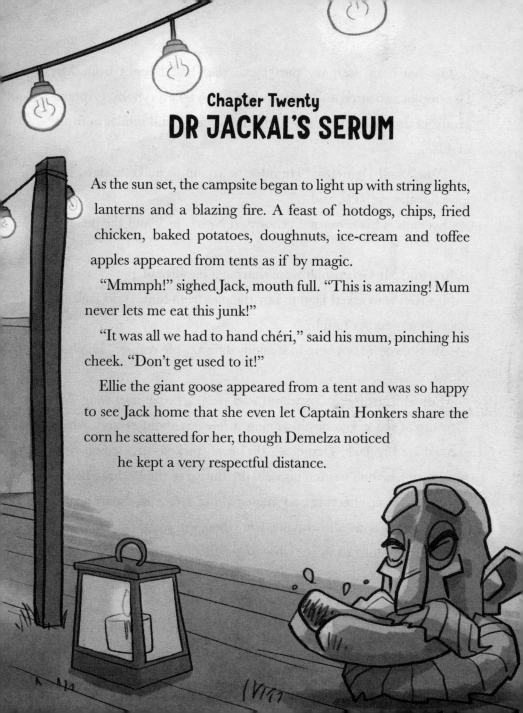

Chapter Twenty
DR JACKAL'S SERUM

As the sun set, the campsite began to light up with string lights, lanterns and a blazing fire. A feast of hotdogs, chips, fried chicken, baked potatoes, doughnuts, ice-cream and toffee apples appeared from tents as if by magic.

"Mmmph!" sighed Jack, mouth full. "This is amazing! Mum never lets me eat this junk!"

"It was all we had to hand chéri," said his mum, pinching his cheek. "Don't get used to it!"

Ellie the giant goose appeared from a tent and was so happy to see Jack home that she even let Captain Honkers share the corn he scattered for her, though Demelza noticed

he kept a very respectful distance.

The batch of stargazy pies Jack's dad had bought from Mr Greensplat appeared and were wolfed down by everybody. Captain Honkers dropped a fish head, with the eyeballs still intact, in front of Ellie.

"Wow," said Demelza, "He must be trying to make friends. He gave her the eyeballs, and…"

"Eyeballs is his favourite!" chorused Nessa, Jack and the pickled knight.

Ren and Mr Greensplat were sharing a big slice of pie.

"It's Ren who asked Dad to buy the pies from him," said Jack. "I guess to remember him by."

"Ah! So, you're not here to steal his stargazy pie recipe?" laughed Nessa.

Musical instruments appeared and people broke into song. Mr Greensplat led everyone in singing a few sea shanties and, when pushed by Big Jack, Demelza's dad even picked up a guitar and sang a song he had written himself, the Ballad of the Bodmin Beast. Seeing everyone cheering and singing along, Demelza wasn't nearly as embarrassed as she usually felt whenever he sang in public. Despite not quite knowing what was going on, or why they were celebrating, he was enjoying the party and Demelza was in no rush for him to take her home and start asking questions. Nessa's mum still looked bemused by the celebrations but had given up trying to grab Nessa for A Word and seemed to be enjoying the party with her crew, especially since Nessa's dad had turned up to join them. Explanations could wait.

A big cheer went up as the main fairground lights came on and the ferris wheel started turning.

"Come on," Jack grabbed their hands and pulled them up. "The other rides still need converting back, but I owe you guys a ferris wheel ride."

Everyone grabbed a cabin on the wheel. Demelza, Nessa and Jack jumped into one together. The pickled knight peered out from the backpack on Nessa's knee as Captain Honkers settled himself next to Demelza. Mr Greensplat and Ren took the cabin behind them, Jack's parents, Demelza's dad and Nessa's parents were all crammed in the one in front.

"Mum can sweet talk anyone," grinned Jack. "I bet you two won't be in nearly so much trouble by the time we've been around once."

"Soooo," Nessa scratched her head awkwardly as the ride started with a jerk. "You're erm, sort of a, y'know… giant?"

"You noticed?" Jack gave a wry smile. He twisted the end of his bandana and sighed. "My Great-great-great grandad believed we needed more power to take down the giants if they woke up. He heard about a doctor near Hyde Park in London who was doing some pretty weird experiments, Dr Jackal, or something like that.

He told the doctor about the giants and together they made a serum using a sample of giant blood. A sip of it could turn you into a giant for a few hours. It was something he was going to save in case we ever needed it, but he tried it out, once. Once was enough. It mutated our bloodline. Since then, the first child born in each generation of our family is part giant."

He looked down at his shoes as if he'd just admitted to eating dogfood sandwiches. Demelza looked at Nessa as the cabin rose slowly above the treetops. Nessa shrugged.

"You can control it though?"

Jack nodded.

"I couldn't when I was very young. Mum would be carrying me on her hip, the next minute I'd be carrying her and Dad like dolls. Dad has it too. He taught me to control it. Now it only happens if I want it to, which is pretty much never."

"I'd use it all the time," said Demelza, her head filling with the possibilities. "I'd scoop up Connan, an' Jory an' Trevik in one hand and threaten to munch and crunch them up with my giant teeth if they ever pushed me around or called me titch again!"

"Maaaybe it's a good thing you don't have giant blood," said Nessa. "Or Jack would have to find you a cave to nap in."

Jack smiled.

"I thought you'd think I was a freak."

"Nothing wrong with being a freak," said Demelza. "Is there, Sir Calenick?" she whispered loudly to Nessa's bag.

"I have no idea what you're talking about," said the pickled knight.

"Ordinary is overrated," said Nessa with a wave of her hand.

The wheel finished its first rotation and their cabin started to rise again. Demelza swung her legs as she looked over the side.

"What happened to the men who tried to take Ren?"

"Dad said when he finally got Ren out of the van, she sang them a forgetting song and they sent them off on the next ferry. But even if they remember and start following us again, it won't matter. Dad agreed, the tapes work so Ren is staying here, with the last of her people." He pointed to the cabin behind them, "And maybe getting back together with an old fiancé."

Nessa and Demelza looked over their shoulders to see Ren and Mr Greensplat holding hands as they gazed out over the starlit sea. Demelza wondered if he still had the ring he was going to give her the night she left.

"Now he can make her Stargazy pie whenever she wants," she smiled.

"He looks so young." said Nessa.

"The magic of Ren," said Jack. "He must have been around that age when they first met. But the smiles on their faces, they're down to you two."

Nessa's backpack shook as it let out a loud cough.

"Sorry, you three," said Jack.

HONK!

"OK-OK! Four."

"What about you?" said Demelza. "Will the Jacks stop travelling too?"

Jack shrugged.

"Dad said we'll need to stay on the road, for a while at least. But we're not completely relying on Ren now, we can make loads of tapes. Maybe someday we'll sell the fair and split managing the sites across the world between the whole crew. We won't need to keep travelling forever."

"You don't look too happy about it," said Demelza as they slowly crested the top of the ride. The wheel stopped for a moment to let someone off and gave them time to gaze out over the whole of Penfurzy. The lights of the harbour town twinkled in the distance. Jack shrugged.

"It's a strange thought. Living in a house. Not moving somewhere new every couple of weeks," he smiled at them, "but it would be cool to have friends like you guys."

"You've got friends like us guys," said Nessa, "we're right here!" She held out her fist and the three of them bumped knuckles.

"All those adventures you've had," said Jack, "that all really happened, right here in Penfurzy?"

"You've seen for yourself," said Nessa, "Penfurzy is full of adventures."

"And ancient treasures!" added Demelza, then sighed. "But adventurers never get to keep the treasure they find."

"Treasure isn't all that special when you've got it," said Jack. "Being happy and having good friends is way better."

"Come back and visit us any time," said Demelza. "We've got spare caravans you can stay in if you want to come to visit Ren… or maybe beat Nessa's high score again,"

"Oi! It was beginner's luck," said Nessa.

"Of course it was," said Jack as they sat back and enjoyed the view. "I bet I can convince Mum and Dad to come this summer. Penfurzy's pretty rad."

"We know," said Demelza as their cabin slowly descended towards the treetops. "We know."

Chapter Twenty-One
HALF A DOZEN EGGS

A week later Demelza was only just starting to make a dent on the huge list of jobs her dad had drawn up to keep her out of mischief for a while. She had even been extra nice to the snot goblins staying in the caravan park and had let them play with some of her old toys. She had only managed to see Nessa once since their adventure as Nessa's mum and dad had been keeping her equally busy. Neither of them had been allowed to go back to fair, but Nessa had suggested that maybe that wasn't too strong a punishment since they'd rowed a rickety old boat through a storm and got trapped in a sea cave without even telling anyone where they were going.

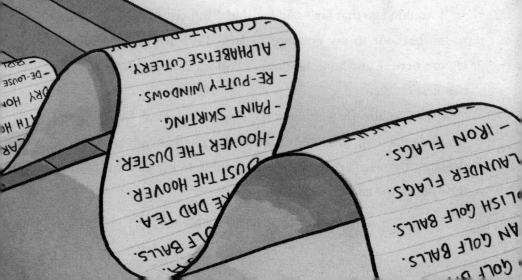

"What I don't understand," Demelza's dad said, as they finished repainting the knights on the first hole of the crazy golf course, "is how you delivered that note to me if you were stuck in a cave?" Demelza was ready for the question.

"Honkers! It was Honkers! I wrote it, an' he grabbed it in his beak an' flew all the way up out of the spout-hole up in the cliffs, an' back here to give it to you, then he flew aaaaall the way back to us."

"Hmmmm," her dad looked at Captain Honkers who was pattering around in circles trying to prune a loose feather from his tail. "That goose right there? You're telling me he flew here, unfolded the note, slid it under the door then knocked loudly, and flew back to you?"

"Errrrrrr, yes," said Demelza as Honkers triumphantly pulled out the feather then staggered dizzily into her dad's legs and fell over. "Um, Dad… seeing as I've been very, very good, and helpful and polite to guests, and tidy…"

"I wouldn't go that far," said her dad. "But yes, I'll take you down to the harbour to say goodbye to Jack. I'll leave Mr Calenick in charge here. I just hope he doesn't end up running around like a headless chicken."

Nessa was already waiting at the dock with Jack as Demelza and her dad pulled up. Most of the fair's lorries had already pulled onto the ferry. Demelza's dad went to say goodbye to Big Jack and Rose as they guided the last lorry on board.

"I guess this is it," said Nessa.

"We'll be back," said Jack. "Ren made us promise to visit at least once a year." He waved over to the pier where Ren and Young Mr Greensplat were sitting sharing an ice-cream as they watched the ferry preparing to leave. Ren blew them all kisses and Mr Greensplat gave them a huge smile.

"Wow, I didn't even know his face could do that!" said Demelza.

"Anyway, I'd better get going," said Jack as his dad waved to him. "I just wanted to say, thank you. From all of us. You saved Penfurzy, maybe the world, and freed us all to have more of a life than just giants. Anyway, we wanted you to have this." he handed them a scrap of paper.

"Your reward has been layed where the turtle once lay," read Demelza. "What is this?"

"Follow the clue and find out," grinned Jack. He threw his arms around them both and gave a big squeeze. "No goodbye's OK? Just, smell you later."

"Smell you later," laughed Nessa and Demelza, as they squeezed him back. They waved him off as he ran back to his parents and onto the ferry, giving one last big wave as the siren sounded and the huge metal doors began to close behind them.

"What does this mean?" said Demelza, reading Jack's note again.

Your reward has been layed where the turtle once lay.

"He spelled layed with a Y instead of L.A.I.D," said Nessa, who was always first to spot spelling mistakes. "Hmm, turtle? He's got to be talking about…"

"Tortuga! Of course," said Demelza. "Where the turtle once lay. Our den in the dunes. Daaaaad," she said as he joined them, "I know you said we have to go straight home, but please-please-please-please-pleeeeeease can me an' Nessa just run up to the dunes to get something? We'll be ten minutes, I promise!"

"Ten minutes," said her dad with a sigh. "I'll be over there talking to Humfra. Don't even dream of running off anywhere else or there'll be…"

"Thaaaaaanks Daaaaaaad!" Demelza called back as she sprinted towards the dunes with Nessa. Down the track, onto the sandy path, over the driftwood fence, through the tall grasses…

"Tortuga," sighed Demelza as they burst through the grass to see their once awesome hideaway reduced to a small dugout slowly being reclaimed by the sand.

"Footprints," said Nessa. They led to the milkcrate table which still sat in the centre of the dugout. "They must be Jack's."

Beneath the crate, on top of their comics and games, was a large eggbox.

"It weighs a ton!" said Nessa as she tried to lift it. "What's he put in it, lead?"

Demelza opened the lid and they both fell back onto their bottoms, staring at the contents of the box. Six very large, very shiny, very heavy…

"Golden eggs," gasped Demelza. She took one and ran her fingers over the smooth golden surface. "How much are these even worth? A million bajillion pounds?"

"Not quite, but a LOT," said Nessa. "Look there's a note in the lid."

Ellie made these especially for you.
A thank you gift, from all of us.
Your friend, Jack

"Ellie?" Nessa looked at Demelza.

"The goose that lays the golden eggs," Demelza gasped. "The one the first Jack stole from the giant at the top of the beanstalk!"

"That was Ellie?" Nessa flopped back into the sand. "She's real! No wonder Jack never seemed bothered about money."

"We're rich," said Demelza. "We can buy a new boat, oh and new tyres for our bikes, and maybe a comic shop…"

"Ooh, and an arcade, and a skatepark for the caravan park!" said Nessa.

"Demellllllzaaaa Penrooooose!" called a voice from way back along the trail.

"Better get up there before your dad adds another month to your sentence," said Nessa.

"Hmm, I have a feeling he's going to get a lot happier, very soon," grinned Demelza as they scooped up the eggs and staggered back up the track.

"You know what this means?" said Nessa as they each held an egg aloft and watched Demelza's dad's face melt into slack-jawed astonishment as the sun glinted off the golden eggs like fiery little suns.

"Sometimes, just sometimes, heroes DO get to keep the treasure."

THE

END

(FOR NOW)

END

(FOR NOW)

GABRIELLE KENT

Gabrielle is from the North East of England. She grew up in the 1980's riding her bike into trouble, drawing monsters, reading comics and playing games on her best friend's Atari. Her first job was in video-games working on games for PC, Playstation and XBox. She taught game design to university students for sixteen years and is now a full time writer. She is the author of the Alfie Bloom series and is excited to be writing books about Nessa and Demelza, stars of the super cool video-game, Knights and Bikes.

LUKE NEWELL

Luke grew up on the suburban border between North East London and Essex: his skill at riding his BMX allowed him to balance right on the border and not fall off once. His favourite things are bike riding and drawing.

Luke has been picture making for over twenty years. He moved through TV animation, to web games, to making PlayStation games with cameras, and shiny helmets with lights on and he continues to do the same thing he's always done, riding bikes, and drawing pictures ... ideally funny ones! Toot toot ding ding!

ACKNOWLEDGEMENTS

I hope you enjoyed reading Nessa and Demelza's latest adventure as much as I enjoyed writing it. Now, this is the bit where I get to say a big THANK YOU to everyone involved.

The Knights and Bikes books are based on the world and characters of the brilliant Knights and Bikes video game created by Rex and Moo, the talented guys behind Foam Sword Games. As always, I'm very grateful to them for letting me play with their world and characters. The rad artwork between these covers is by Luke Newell who is always hiding funny little jokes and secrets in his pictures. I love working with Luke, his artwork is as energetic and exciting as Nessa and Demelza and I'm always very excited to see it.

Thank you to my wonderful agent, Hannah Sheppard, and my publishers, Knights Of, particularly my editor Eishar Brar for her great advice, design ace Marssaié, and to David Stevens for asking me to write these books in the first place. Thank you to my forever supportive husband, Satish, especially for keeping our wonderful daughter occupied long enough for me to actually get this book written, and to my family for all of their support and cheerleading.

Sending air high-fives, from a safe social distance, to all of the brilliant librarians, teachers, and booksellers who have been sharing the world of Penfurzy with readers like you. So many people are involved in getting a book from my head into your hands. Thank you to them, and to you for joining us on this adventure. I hope you enjoyed hanging out on Penfurzy. Please come again soon!

- Gabrielle Kent

My thanks go out to everybody at Knights Of, you really are shining valiant heroes. To the immediate team that I worked with on this: Marssaié for your excellent design and flexibility in melding things together. David for spinning the plates, with a smile and unmatched generosity of spirit.

To Gabrielle, whose words genuinely made me laugh, and cry, thanks for allowing me to ride tandem on the journey of transposing the game world to the page. If it's un-nerving me 'seeing into your brain', try not to be so good at putting your brain into words!

Special thanks to Rex, and Moo, at Foam Sword, the giants whose shoulders I've ridden around on...for letting me mess about in your world, and again, allowing the slightly skewed, alternate reality from your BEAUTIFUL game find it's own shape. You happy? Me happy.

I send enormous thanks to my wife Claire, without whose support all this would be impossible. It's often our time together that we both sacrifice so I can scratch out funny pictures. Not an hour of this goes unappreciated. All love to you, forever.

I'll extend these thanks to my two wonderful daughters Vera and Iris.

Thanks for your various bikes, toys, poses and faces that have been folded into the pages of these books. They are time capsules of you, of moments that in time I know I will forget... but bookmarked, if you will.

- Luke Newell

ME AND NESSA HOPE YOU ENJOYED OUR ADVENTURE WHAT GABRIELLE WROTE DOWN IN THIS **BOOK!!**

BUT THERES A WHOLE OTHER STORY (THAT YOU CAN PLAY!) IN THE KNIGHTS AND BIKES VIDEO GAME!!

YOU CAN FEED CAPTAIN HONKERS!

YOU CAN RIDE AROUND ON BIKES!

SCARE AWAY THE BADDIES!

YOU CAN EVEN USE MY GAME-GAUNTLET AND IT'S MAGICKAL POWERS!!

AND YOU CAN PLAY IT ON YOUR OWN, BUT IT'S EVEN BETTER WITH A FRIEND!

KNIGHTS AND BIKES

IT'S OUT NOW FOR NINTENDO SWITCH AND PLAYSTATION 4 AND PC AND MAC!